[1. Paranormal Cozy Mystery — Fiction. 2. Cozy Mystery —
Fiction. 3. Amateur Sleuths — Fiction. 4. Female Sleuth —
Fiction. 5. Wit and Humor — Fiction.] 1. Title.

TRIXIE SILVERTALE

PEPPERMINT COOKIE MURDER

Christmas Catastrophe Mysteries

Sittin' On A Goldmine Productions, L.L.C.

pr@sittinonagoldmine.co

www.sittinonagoldmine.co

This is a work of fiction. Names, characters, places, and incidents are products of the author's imagination or are used fictitiously and are not to be construed as real. Any resemblance to actual events, locales, business establishments, organizations, or persons, living or dead, is entirely coincidental.

ISBN: 978-1-952739-22-4

Cover Design © Sittin' On A Goldmine Productions, L.L.C.

Trixie Silvertale
Peppermint Cookie Murder: Paranormal Cozy Mystery : a novel / by Trixie Silvertale — 1st ed.

INTRODUCTION TO THIS HOLIDAY MYSTERY!

When Santa's daughter leaves the North Pole on a baking quest, will her sweet dreams turn fatally sour?

Cindy Claus is excited to open her own bakery. She's determined to pursue her passion and have her holiday treats prove she's more than a Yuletide heir. But before she can whisk up a success, her roommate is murdered and Cindy is the prime suspect.

With finding the real killer the only way to beat the rap, Cindy relies on the kindness of strangers and her father's trusted arctic fox. But without a recipe for success in the unfamiliar human world, grilling the wrong suspects could put her behind bars...

Can Cindy sift out the clues before she's done and dusted?

Peppermint Cookie Murder is the first book in the festive paranormal cozy series, Christmas Catastrophe Mysteries. If you like kind-hearted heroines, furry sidekicks, and a dash of mistletoe magic, then you'll love Trixie Silvertale's tasty whodunit.

Enjoy *Peppermint Cookie Murder* and cook up a frenzy today!

Features recipes from Cindy's bakery!

CHAPTER 1

The chorus of "O Come, All Ye Faithful" echoes from the peppermint-striped speaker next to my bed. Groaning, I pull a pillow over my head.

With less than a week left until Christmas, my father pulls the reindeer reins tight. Not a single resident of our North Pole home may sleep past 5:00 a.m.

The next song to crackle from the loudspeaker is "Jingle Bells."

I know if I don't get up by the end of this song, one of my father's platoons of elves will be in to fetch me.

Screaming silently, I throw my pillow at the door.

Unfortunately, at that exact moment, my mother opens that door.

"Cynthia Cherubim Claus! What on earth did I do to deserve that?"

I bolt upright in bed, and my round cheeks feel as red as my hair.

"Mama, I'm so sorry. It wasn't aimed at you. I was—"

"You're upset about the wake-up call. I understand, Marshmallow. I know this last big push before Christmas is always hard on you. But you've got to get used to it. You'll be starting your official training on December 26th. Your father will expect you to run this marathon-to-Christmas next year, when you're head of the company."

Gazing at the floor, I kick my feet back and forth from my perch on the edge of the bed. "What if I'm not ready, Mama?"

"Nonsense! You'll be a hundred and fifteen this Christmas. Your father is so looking forward to retiring. You've got to step up. He thinks he'll always be here to help you — but in a few centuries . . . Listen, dear, your father has been doing this for nearly a thousand years. And he loves this job as much today as he did the first night he ever delivered toys. He wants to share that joy with you. You can understand that, can't you?"

My mother's beautiful elvish features beam

with pride and hope. Her sparkling green eyes gaze so deeply into mine, I'm afraid she can see my very soul.

Hopefully not.

My heart isn't in it. I've known for at least a decade, but I didn't have the courage to tell anyone. When you grow up with Santa Claus as your father, there's not a lot of wiggle room in your career path.

"I'll make a deal with you, Mama. If you promise to tell me my favorite bedtime story tonight, I'll paste a smile on my face and get through this day without complaint."

"Oh Cindy, you're too old for bedtime stories." Mother adjusts her shimmering blonde ponytail and pulls me to my feet. "Now get dressed, and after breakfast, we'll take a little run. Sound good?"

Sounds terrible! My mother was rumored to be nearly two thousand years old. However, she looks younger than me. Elves aren't immortal, but they have exceedingly long life spans. Despite her innate magic and near immortality, my mother has always taken exceptional care of what she refers to as her "vessel." She's never had more than one cookie after supper, and she wouldn't dream of placing over five marshmallows in her hot chocolate.

"I don't feel like a run, Mama. I'll be down for breakfast in five. Can I have gingerbread cookies?"

"Cynthia! Cookies . . . for breakfast? I don't care what your father says, that's not healthy. He may be fattening up for his big sleigh ride, but I thought you and I had agreed to put a new face on the holiday when you took over? You know, healthy holidays and all that."

No response required. Mother and I have disagreed about absolutely everything since I could speak. I love her, don't get me wrong. We just don't see eye to eye. Even though I'm technically half elf, some days it feels like I'm more my father's daughter than hers.

"See you at the breakfast table, Mother."

She exhales softly as she leaves.

In my spacious bathroom, I wash my face and comb my bone-straight red hair. My father claims his hair was as red as mine when he was a teenager. But it turned snow white on his twentieth birthday, and it's been that way ever since.

Everyone assumed the same thing would happen to me. Here I am, a hundred and fifteen, with hair as fiery red as the day I was born.

After wadding my hair into a messy bun, I throw on a white sweatshirt with an ironic picture of my father on the front, and red sweatpants. I can't see the point of dressing up. We never go anywhere. I have literally never been outside our magical village in my entire life.

At the breakfast table, my father and his most trusted advisor, Artikoa, have their heads close together at the far end of the table.

My mother has prepared an egg-white omelette for me, with a glass of orange juice and half a slice of toast. Apparently, my behavior did not earn me a gingerbread cookie.

Not to worry. There's a chunky elf called Cinnamon Roll that runs the local bakery. It was my first after-school job, and we always kept in touch. I still go in and help her out in the off-season. I'll swing by and grab myself a treat on the way to the plant.

Artikoa yips to get my attention.

Gazing toward my father's end of the table, I endure a glare from the arctic fox. He pinches his eyelids to mere slits. "Good morning, Cynthia. Your father tells me you will run the morning inventory check at the plant. Shall I accompany you?"

I'd rather eat an egg-white omelette. Of course, I don't say this out loud. "That would be lovely, Artikoa. I have a couple of errands to run on my way. Shall I meet you there at six?"

He angles his pointed nose toward the grandfather clock next to the sideboard. "That's forty-five minutes from now. It's only a five-minute walk. What business could you have that would keep you away from the plant? Inventory should begin at 5:30."

Stacks of snowballs! "I can run my errands later. We can walk over now if you like."

He hops from the chair in a puff of snow-white grace. "Wonderful. Lead the way, Princess."

Before you get concerned that he's a chauvinist or perhaps talking down to me, I literally am a princess. My mother, Erregina, is an elf queen. But we don't need to get into that right now.

I lead the way from our cozy home and step outside into the carefully controlled climate of our magical village. The cobblestone streets seem to glow in the sunlight, warming through the magical dome that protects us. My mother created an elaborate system to redirect the sun's rays from far south. Otherwise, we would be in almost total darkness during our busiest season.

As we pass the bakery, the scent of gingerbread and all the other delights nearly stops me in my tracks.

"Is something amiss, Cynthia?" Artikoa pauses and looks up at me with those piercing, all-knowing, amber eyes.

"Not a thing. Will I be working with Ginger or Anise on the inventory?"

"Ginger was moved to acquisitions last month. You should know that. Anise will be the primary contact today."

Blizzards! Every time I open my mouth around this fox, I feel like a helpless newborn bunny.

When we walk through the front doors of the factory, every elf in sight turns and waves a happy greeting. I appreciate their positivity; I really do. I'm just not that excited about this line of work. As heir to Santa's kingdom, I could've had literally any toy a girl could want. Instead, I spent my entire life collecting books and maps. When I learned that there were places outside the North Pole, and my father got to visit all of them every year, I dreamed of traveling.

At first, my parents thought it was a genuine interest in my father's business, but it wasn't. I didn't want to deliver toys all over the world. I only wanted to *see* the world. So I collected maps and read the names of faraway countries as I imagined what it must be like in each of those mysterious places.

Artikoa gave one of his classic yips, and I glanced down at the elf in front of me. "Oh, hi Anise. Are you ready to get started?"

"Yes, Miss Claus. I have everything prepared.

We're on a tight schedule! The production—" She swallows hard, slowly blinks, and takes a deep breath.

Elves aren't able to lie. They can hide the truth, but they can't tell an outright lie. This one is definitely trying to hide something.

"What's wrong, Anise? Is there a problem we need to solve?"

Every elf I've ever known loves to solve problems. She smiles brightly. "Yes. We're a little behind schedule in electronics. The order volume is higher than ever this year, and we've only retrained about one-fifth of our wooden toy makers to join manufacturing."

I'm sure my father expected this. "How far behind are we? We should be at about ninety-eight percent, right?"

She swallows hard and tugs at the pointed tip of one ear. "Well, we're at eighty-five percent."

"What? We have less than a week until Christmas, Anise. How do you plan to complete fifteen percent of our work in six days? I don't want to be the one to share this news with Santa. Do you?"

She smiles nervously. "Perhaps you could speak to your mother?"

Of course. Every time something goes wrong, my mother's magic is meant to solve it. They act like they don't have any magic of their own. I can't understand where their reluctance comes from. "Anise, my mother has much more important things to manage for the village. Like our entire climate. Why don't you speak to the head of the department, and between the two of you, I'm sure you'll find the magic you need to get back on track before Santa has to get involved."

"Yes, miss. I'm sure you're right. What was I thinking?" She tugs the tip of her pointed ear once again and practically runs toward the candy-cane-striped elevator.

Artikoa rests on his haunches and seems to smile. "Your father said you were coming into your own. I had doubted him, but that was assertive instruction. You are becoming a formidable boss. Next time, you needn't mention your father as a threat. However, he will be pleased to receive this report."

My shoulders droop, and I shuffle toward the office to update the inventory.

"What's the matter, Cynthia?"

"I don't like being assertive, Artikoa. I enjoy being kind. I enjoy giving gifts and sleeping past 5:00 a.m.!" Without updating the inventory, I spin on the heels of my red satin boots and march out the door.

My father's advisor is left with his mouth open and his pink tongue hanging out like a misplaced strip of taffy.

Let him deal with the inventory issues. I'm going to get a gingerbread cookie!

Hustling up the cobblestone street, I glimpse my mother and her entourage approaching from the other direction.

Darting into the tailor's, I duck behind a rack of smocks.

Elves have excellent hearing, so the shopkeeper prances from the back room, grinning eagerly. "Miss Claus. What an honor. What can I make for you on this day?"

"Oh, no. I'm not here—" My mother's commanding voice echoes off the cobblestone as she and her hangers-on sweep past.

With a sigh of relief, I step toward the door, completely forgetting my manners.

"Miss Claus? Did I offend?"

"What? No, Thimble. You're magnificent. I'm not sure what I thought I needed. There's bound to be a holiday party or two coming up . . . I bet I'll think of something, though. See you soon."

Hustling out the door, I practically run down the street, hoping to get to the bakeshop without making a further fool of myself.

As I open the door, I inhale deeply and smile with all the love in my heart.

Cinnamon Roll dusts the flour off her hands and steps from behind the counter. "Cindy! What a wonderful holiday surprise!"

CHAPTER 2

THE COMFORT OF THE FAMILIAR space and all the welcoming aromas instantly calm my racing heart and mind. It feels like a weight has been lifted, if only for a moment.

The stout elf grins. "What can I get you?"

"May I please have three gingerbread cookies with extra icing on the side?" I make little fists and bounce on my tiptoes in anticipation.

Cinnamon Roll opens the case and selects three of the most perfect, chewy gingerbread cookies. Then she pulls her piping bag from the cooler and fills a small sugar-cookie cup with extra icing.

"Three gingerbread cookies usually mean a bad

day, dearie. Why don't you tell ol' Cinnamon Roll all about it."

Gratefully accepting the plate of cookies, I plunk onto a stool at the counter. Before I can find the strength to respond, I take a large bite of my first treat. "These are the best!"

Cinnamon Roll pours herself a cup of coffee and fills a mug with hot chocolate and marshmallows for me.

By the time she slides the festive beverage in front of me, I'm ready to talk.

"Remember when I used to work here after school?"

The jolly elf sips her coffee and brushes flour from her apron. "Like it was yesterday. You were the best little worker I ever hired. If I could get even one of my employees to care about baking as much as you did . . ." Cinnamon Roll wags her head back and forth and takes another sip of coffee.

Popping the rest of the second cookie into my mouth, I follow it with a swig of hot chocolate and nod my agreement. "I miss those days, CR. Everything was so simple. I worked hard in school, came here afterward, and then I slept like an ancient elf every night. Now, I don't know what I want to do with my life, and I can't sleep for more than two hours stitched together. My life is a mess."

"How could it possibly be a mess? Your father tells me you're doing great down at the factory. You start your official apprenticeship the day after Christmas, right?"

I roll my eyes and savor the last of the icing. "But my heart's not in it. What's wrong with me? I'm Santa's daughter. Why don't I want to deliver toys to all the girls and boys?"

CR reaches into the pastry case, retrieves a perfect peppermint cookie, and places it on my plate.

"Your secret recipe?"

She winks. "You're the only person besides me who knows that recipe."

This amazing baker makes her dough extra fudgy and smashes up real candy canes to get an authentic peppermint kick. "Your secret's safe with me. Although, I did make them at home one time. Hope that's okay."

"It's more than okay, dearie! You've earned the right to make any of my recipes. Now tell me what's turned your nose up at toys."

I wouldn't dare tell any other elf in the North Pole how I truly felt, but CR and I have a special bond. It's a good feeling to know I can trust her with the truth.

"I love helping people. And there's nothing wrong with toys — technically. I just don't have any passion for the work. My father's so excited every year! It puts a lot of pressure on a gal."

She fills my hot chocolate and mulls over my words. "Have you talked to your father about this?"

My eyes widen, and I struggle to swallow. "Tell Santa his daughter is a fraud?"

CR reaches a pudgy hand across the counter and pats my arm. "Oh now, don't say that. You're just different. Your father has a special connection to toys — he always has. Tell him the truth. What's the worst that could happen?"

I choke on my cocoa. A marshmallow flies out of my mouth and lands on the counter. I try to catch my breath and apologize, but Cinnamon Roll just wipes the marshmallow away with her apron, laughing until tears leak from her deep-blue elf eyes. "Oh, dearie me. I haven't laughed that hard since — since you and I worked together. It sure is good to see you, Cindy. Take it from a parent. You need to be honest with your papa. I know he's Santa, and you don't want to end up on the Naughty List, but telling a lie, or, worse yet, living a lie, will get you on that list faster than you can say double-fudge brownie!"

She's right. I know she's right. But I don't have to like it.

"Thank you for all the delicious treats. I'll think about what you said. Now I better get back to the plant before Artikoa runs home and tattles on me."

CR packages up three more peppermint cookies, in a sweet gingham napkin, and slides them across the counter to me. "How is that sly old fox?"

"As bossy as ever! The only good thing about taking over the toy business will be appointing my own advisors."

She chuckles, and I thank her again for the parting gift as I exit the beloved bakery and trudge back to the factory.

The steady whir of machinery and the merry songs of the workers lift my spirits, if only until the end-of-shift bells jingle. This time of year, the elves work around the clock. Some of them love to keep on a swing or starlight schedule. I'm pleased I only have to stay for the day. Although, if I can't fix my insomnia problem, maybe I'll start working the night shift with the rest of the stargazers.

When I reach home, magnificent aromas fill the air. My mother is making one of her Basque specialties. A layered vegetable dish with a delicious gravy made from reindeer milk, marjoram, smoked paprika, anise seed, and flakes from a special dried pepper my father procures for her every Christmas Eve.

Years ago, my papa chose to be a vegetarian. My mother's strong connection to nature and animals had led her down that path from birth. Father grew up in a poor village where they ate whatever they could get their hands on, but he was happy to make the change. Occasionally, there will be fish or seafood, but for the most part we stick to the vegetables, legumes, and grains we grow in our local gardens, as well as fresh-made bread and pasta.

Despite the luscious smells, Father and Artikoa are absent from supper.

Catching my mother's eye, I nod toward the other end of the table and shrug.

"Your father said there was a problem at the plant. Something they had to handle immediately. I offered my assistance, of course, but he assured me he and his elven managers would work things out. I'm keeping a plate warm for him." She gestures to our cozy kitchen and smiles. "How was your day at the factory?"

I have always found it easier to talk to my mother, rather than my father, about my feelings. Something about her disarming gaze and melodic voice . . . She knows how to draw the truth from me — even when we don't agree.

"Mama, I have to tell you something important. Promise you won't be mad?"

The elven queen shifts in her chair and weaves her long, elegant fingers together. Then, calmly placing her hands on the table, she exhales lightly.

"You know you can tell me anything, Cynthia. I love you no matter what."

And I believe her. As I've believed every time she said that for the last hundred and fifteen years.

"I don't want to take over the business. I don't want to deliver toys."

She gasps, and her carefully folded hands fly to her chest. "What? When did this happen?"

"Mama, this is how I've always felt. I was afraid to tell you."

"I knew you felt uneasy. It would be hard for anyone to fill your father's boots. Not even I—" A single tear rolls down her flawless cheek.

Jumping from my chair, I run to her side and put my arms tightly around her. "Oh, please don't cry. Please don't cry. I'll talk to father tonight. I'm going to ask him to cut a door."

My mother's tears instantly cease. Her emerald-green eyes shift to stormy grey, and she rattles her head in confusion. "A door? You mean to leave the North Pole? To abandon your family?"

She rises from her chair and, despite her diminutive stature, seems to tower over me. "I will not allow this. It is unheard of!"

I hadn't been sure until I spoke the words out loud, but now I feel an unquenchable thirst in my soul. I have to explore the world. Not just one night a year. Not just to deliver toys. I want to go live among humans and find my passion — carve my own path.

SITTING ALONE AT THE DINING ROOM TABLE picking at my food is not how I wanted my father to find me, but Santa does as Santa pleases.

"Cindy? I hope you weren't waiting on me for supper."

"No, Papa." Before I can offer any additional explanation, tears sluice down my cheeks.

My father instantly drops to one knee and scoops his arms around me. His fluffy beard always smells of peppermint and reminds me of the delicious cookies I—

"I have to tell you something. I know you're going to be upset. Mama was furious, but I have to tell you. It hurts too much to continue keeping it inside."

He pulls out the chair next to me, takes a seat, and leans forward — listening as though I'm the only person in the world.

"If you're going to tell me what you want for Christmas, I already have a pretty good idea."

His sweet attempt to lighten my mood falls flat. Taking the napkin from my lap, I wipe my tears and twist in my seat to face him. "I'm not taking over the family business, Papa. Toys are your passion, not mine."

The hurt in his eyes is almost more than I can bear, but I've said this much, and I have to finish. "I want you to cut a door. I need to go out into the real world and find my way. I can't do it here with all these expectations of things that were decided when I was too little to tell you how I felt."

I've certainly never experienced anything more painful than watching Santa cry. To know that those tears were my fault only makes this experience worse.

"Papa! Please don't. I'll visit you and Mama. And you'll visit me — every year on Christmas Eve. You won't put me on the Naughty List, will you?"

His arms circle around me in an instant, and he holds me in a polar-bear hug for far too long. I can scarcely breathe, but I refuse to pull away. If he can accept my choice and still love me, I will absolutely almost suffocate for that.

"My sweet Cherubim, I knew this day was coming. I told myself I could stop it. I told myself it was only a phase, but deep in my heart, I knew you were unhappy here. Let me talk to your mother. I can bring her around. Plus, I'll need the help of her magic to open a door for you, my dear. Where are we sending you?"

"I don't know. I never thought you'd allow it." And tears are once again flooding my cheeks.

"The three of us will have breakfast together tomorrow. No Artikoa. No other elves. Just the family. Why don't you take a look at one of the many maps you've collected over the years and pick a place that sounds inviting? We can make all the arrangements tomorrow. Will you be leaving before Christmas?" His voice catches in his throat.

"I— I have to, Papa. I have to go before I lose my nerve. In my whole life, I've never been without you and Mama. I'm not sure I can do it on my own, but something inside tells me I have to try."

He kisses the top of my head as he stands, and his beard tickles my skin. "I'll see you in the morning, Marshmallow."

Santa disappears up the staircase at the north end of the house — the wing he shares with my mother.

After clearing the table, washing the dishes, and putting the leftovers in the icebox, I pad softly up to my room to pull my magic globe from the top shelf of my closet.

Spinning the globe, I stop it with one finger. Wherever my finger lands, a small bubble appears, like a snow globe, and shows me what's happening at that very spot right now.

Part of me longs to visit somewhere warm and tropical, but I have lived my whole life in the snow. The northern lights, snowflakes, icicles, even blizzards. Visiting the human world will be tough enough. I better at least pick a climate I understand.

As I continue to spin the globe and explore possibilities, the aurora borealis seems to pulse with an excitement that matches my own. When the handle on my door twists, I turn expectantly.

"I promised you a bedtime story, Marshmallow. Is it too late?"

"It's never too late, Mama!"

Rushing toward her, I wrap her in a warm embrace. She returns the hug, and we cuddle together on my large round bed.

Her magical voice is soft and clear. "Once upon a time, there was a toymaker with a small shop in the Dolomites in Carezza, Val d'Ega."

I squeeze my mother's hand, encouraging her to continue.

"The toymaker had lost his wife in childbirth. His only son was his most prized creation."

It warms my heart to think I'm my mama and papa's most prized creation.

CHAPTER 3

*M*y eyelids are growing heavy, and I'm not sure I'll make it to the end. As a small child, I remember falling asleep within minutes. Tonight feels different. I feel like part of the story . . . part of my family's future.

Mama continues, her melodic voice painting images as she speaks. "The toymaker's son worked tirelessly to create unique and magnificent toys for their village."

I've heard this story countless times in my brief life, and occasionally, I can't resist sharing a tidbit. "Did the toymaker teach his son everything he knew?"

My mother smiles and squeezes my hand. "Yes, and the toymaker told his son that the boy had a gift for making toys. Some of the boy's ideas seemed impossible, but right in front of the aging toymaker's eyes, the creations would come to life.

"One morning, when the son entered the workshop, he found his father slumped over the toy bench, appearing to be fast asleep. The boy was unconcerned. His father had a habit of falling asleep in the workshop. But today, when he shook his father's shoulder, it was cold, and his father did not respond."

"What did the boy do, Mama?"

"The boy of sixteen was forced to bury his father in a pauper's grave, but he did not let that hardship steal his love of toy making. He doubled his efforts, and two weeks later, on Christmas Eve, he honored his father's memory the best way he knew how. He stuffed each toy in an old flour sack and, in the dead of night, he slipped into his neighbors' homes to place special toys on each hearth.

"Now that village was filled with trusting folk who didn't lock their doors, and since the young man's mission was the selfless spreading of joy, no harm came to him.

"In the morning, when all the children discovered their toys, cheers drifted from the windows, and the parents claimed blessings from above. Gifts from a true saint." She pauses and catches my eye.

"They didn't know he really was a saint. His mom had been an angel, right?"

My mother kisses my cheek and wipes a tear from her eye. "That's right. An angel had fallen in love with the toymaker and his passion for spreading cheer. They conceived a child, and when the child was born, the angel — even though it broke her heart — had to return to heaven. From above, she watched over the kindhearted toymaker and their precious child. She mourned the loss of the toymaker, but rejoiced when she saw the kindness her son shared with the world. 'Saint' eventually became 'Santa,' and she knew all her sacrifices had been worth it."

"Can you skip to the part where he discovers that his angelic heritage gives him the power to stop time when he does good deeds, and then he meets the woman in the woods?"

My mother chuckles softly and pats my hand. "Several years later, after the young man's hair had turned snowy white and genuine happiness had added weight to his frame, he crept into a small cottage deep in the forest. He had begun to hire other toymakers to help him make more gifts, and, at this point in time, he delivered toys to most of Europe each Christmas Eve. Every year, he expanded his deliveries farther and discovered new families in need of kindness."

"Back to the cottage, Mama." I squeeze her arm in anticipation.

"On this night, he walked softly toward a split-rock fireplace to leave a toy. Before he could lay the gift on the hearth, a woman stepped from the shadows and threatened him with her broom. 'Who goes there?'

"The white-haired man froze in confusion. 'You can see me? Why has time not stopped in this cottage?'

"The woman tilted her flaxen-haired head and pondered the many rumors she had heard over the years. She lowered her broom and moved bravely toward the intruder. 'What is your name?'

"He squared his shoulders and looked deep into her emerald-green eyes. 'On this night, I'm called Santa.'

"The slender woman gazed at the man she believed had been a myth. 'You are the toymaker's son?'

"He swallowed and looked away. 'I prefer Santa.'

"'I prefer Santa as well.' She reached out and gripped his hand. 'My people have taken shelter in this woodland. We are under attack from a barbarian tribe from the East. I know of a place we can all be safe, together. My people love to create.

It would bring them joy to make toys for you. Will you join me?'"

"Can I say what happens next?" Without waiting for my mother to answer, I sit up and recite the end of the story by heart. "The elven queen and the toymaker called Santa moved to the North Pole, where her magic protects them to this day."

My mother hugs me and whispers softly. "And they had a child of their own who would grow up to follow her heart and exceed all their expectations."

She pulls me close, and I'm sound asleep in her embrace when my father discovers us in the morning.

"I thought I might find my two favorite girls here." He takes a seat on the edge of the bed and puts his large hand around ours. "I made chocolate-chip pancakes and peppermint cocoa for breakfast. Plus, I picked up a few peppermint cookies at the bakery." Papa winks at me, and my mother throws her hands in the air and scoffs. "I will never make any headway with my plans for healthy holidays. You two share the same obsession with sweets."

Shrugging my shoulders, I return my father's wink. "Must come from the angel side, right, Papa?"

He smiles warmly and helps my mother to her feet. "It certainly must."

We all traipse down to the breakfast table, and father sets a warm carafe of maple syrup next to my plate.

"Can I also have whipped cream?"

He laughs openly and fetches a bowl of whipped goodness he had already prepared from the icebox.

"Tell us where you've decided to travel, Cindy."

My father shoves a large forkful of chocolate-chip pancakes into his mouth, and my mother lifts a napkin quickly to hide the sadness on her face.

"I'd like to try a place called Silver Shoals, Papa. The climate is similar to here, and it's a small enough town. I won't be overwhelmed."

He nods and smiles. "What project will you try first?"

Twisting the napkin in my lap, I bite my bottom lip and work to settle my tumbling tummy. "I'm going to open a bakery."

Erregina's eyes widen with shock, but she says nothing.

My father pats his round belly and grins. "Don't forget to leave out a plate of cookies for me on Christmas Eve."

His laughter fills the room, and eventually, my mother warms to the idea. We discuss all the possibilities of what I might bake and sell at my establishment. With little trouble at all, we agree that a "Christmas year-round" theme would be a wonderful addition to any town. I plan to include basics like fresh bread and a variety of muffins, but my specialty would be Christmas sweet treats.

"What do you think I should call it, Papa?"

My mother offers a suggestion or two that are all quite practical, but don't catch the spirit of what I'm after. Cindy's Bakeshop gets the point across, but I'd hoped for more pizzazz. Finally, my father wipes the whipped cream from his beard and his dark eyes twinkle. "Yuletide Me Over Bakery."

Jumping to my feet, I smile and clap my hands. "Oh, Papa! It's perfect. Yuletide Me Over Bakery! I love it."

After a second helping of pancakes, I push my chair back from the table. As I kiss my father's rosy cheek and thank him for the wonderful meal, he takes my hand in his.

"Cindy, there's a great deal you don't know about the human world. To start with, there are a lot of steps involved in opening a business. I'm going to send Artikoa along as your advisor. He'll keep you safe and make sure your bakery is set up properly."

"What?" I couldn't believe it. Before I had even

set one foot outside the North Pole, my father was saddling me with a spy!

Without a word, I grab the last peppermint cookie from the platter on the table and run out the front door.

At first, I head toward the bakery, but when I reach that point on the cobblestone road, I keep going. I run past the tailor's, the factory, and the gardens.

As I pass through the livestock barn, I can feel the magic shifting. By the time I emerge into the reindeer paddock, snow covers the ground, and elves bundled in cozy winter sweaters attend to Santa's most treasured friends.

When my mother and father relocated to the North Pole, they explored a multitude of options for Christmas Eve transportation. Opening magical portals to each and every home in the world, even with their abilities, was too over the top. Plus, it would've seriously drained them of magic. My father doubted if it was even an option.

The elves communed with local ice spirits and dryads who spoke of sturdy, gentle creatures outside the dome.

My father and twelve trusted elven elders cut a door in our dome and left to explore the possibilities. Of course, Artikoa also accompanied them on the mission. His ancient wisdom and the ability to speak the language of all animals would be useful.

Initially, the reindeer herds were fearful of the fox. My father added his calming, jovial energy to the exchange, and in a few hours, the elves and reindeer were discussing workable options.

Purely by accident, my father approached one of the largest stags and stroked the buck's head.

At my father's touch, the beast floated off the tundra, wild-eyed and braying.

Artikoa eventually calmed the buck, and after several tests, it was discovered that my father's pure love and desire to deliver toys to all the girls and boys somehow translated to flight in these majestic beasts.

An alliance was formed between the North Pole kingdom and the herds of wild reindeer.

Each year, twelve new reindeer, bucks and does, were chosen to join Santa's herd. They would enter the dome and become part of the North Pole village.

They lived in exquisite comfort and chose mates at will, returning to the wilderness when they retired.

If their population within our humble village ever exceeded our maximum capacity, word would be sent to the reindeer that no recruits were needed that year.

As I trudge through the knee-deep snow in the paddock, several of the reindeer lift their heads from mangers filled with hay and move toward me.

Without the aid of Artikoa to translate, I won't be able to have a direct conversation. However, I can spill all my troubles without any concern for repercussions.

As I explain my frustration over fighting for my independence only to be rewarded by my father hanging a spy on my coattails, the rest of the herd encircles me.

I reach a hand toward the nearest doe and stroke her coarse fur.

Nothing happens. For a split second, I'm disappointed.

Not sure what I was hoping for, but perhaps if my touch had caused the animal to take flight, I would've been forced to rethink my decision.

Since nothing of the kind happens, it confirms leaving is the right thing for me.

This is an important step in my life, and I'm not willing to give up. If my only way out is to take a sly fox along for the ride, I suppose I'll have to take the good with the bad.

Besides, my father didn't say I had to listen to everything that Artikoa says. He only said I had to take him with me.

Done.

After thanking the reindeer herd for their polite listening, I return to the barn to grab a scoop of dried lichen and scatter it across the snowy field. Several of the reindeer nod their heads in what appears to be thanks, and I trudge toward home.

The table has been cleared, and the kitchen stands empty.

Perhaps I've finally pushed my parents too far. Today was supposed to be an excellent opportunity to make plans for my trip. Maybe my behavior has changed their minds. I couldn't blame them if it had. At the first sign of trouble, I stormed off like a seventy-five-year-old elf. Things aren't going to be easy in the human world — I've heard the stories.

When I reach my bedroom, the door is closed. Strange. I don't remember doing that.

Twisting the handle, I push the door open and find my mother perched on my bed and my father seated on the desk with the magic globe beside him.

"Have you changed your mind, Cindy?"

"No. I apologize for my behavior. You were right to think I might need a guide. And I'll be grateful for the connection to home that Artikoa will provide."

My father's knowing smile says everything he

refuses to speak out loud. "I've taken a look at Silver Shoals. It suits you."

The cloud of mistrust vanishes, and my excitement returns. "Do you mean it? I'm going to miss you and Mama terribly, but I'm so excited!"

My mother moves toward my father and glances at the globe.

"Have you packed your things?"

My face falls slack, and it feels as though my mother can read my mind.

She reaches her hand toward the sapphire amulet around her neck and rubs it once in a clockwise circle.

Beside me, a large trunk, three roomy suitcases, and a small wooden chest appear.

"There. That should hold you over nicely, Marshmallow."

Blinking back tears of joy, I take a deep breath. "I'm ready. Should we send someone to—?"

A yip echoes from the hallway, and Artikoa pads into the room, leaps onto my bed, and sits proudly with this fluffy tail curled around his feet. "I received your summons, sir. How may I assist?"

My father gives him a matter-of-fact summary of the events and decisions that have transpired since yesterday.

By the expression on the fox's face, I'd venture to say he's no more pleased about the arrangement than I. To his credit, he makes no such comment aloud.

Okay, I can definitely learn something from him.

My father places his finger on the globe, at the point called Silver Shoals, and reaches his other hand toward my mother. She grips his outstretched hand firmly and places her left hand upon her sapphire amulet.

Faster than a snowflake melting on my father's cheek, Artikoa and I are no longer in the North Pole.

CHAPTER 4

"Where are we?" I glance left and right at the unfamiliar room. An antique brass bed stands near the window, draped with a cheery quilt. To my right are two cozy, overstuffed chairs and, beyond them, a small kitchen and a sturdy oak table with two chairs.

Artikoa jogs the perimeter, sniffing high and low. "Your father made some arrangements."

"What? I can't believe this! He doesn't think I'll be able to do this. He has no faith in me."

The wise fox leaps onto a green-velvet chair and inhales sharply. "On the contrary, Cynthia. Your father wants you to have the best possible chance for success. You asked him to transport you and all of your—" He points his nose toward the trunk, suitcases, and small chest. "Did you expect him to drop you in the middle of the street in a strange town? That would hardly put your best foot forward. He made arrangements for you to have a place to live above your bakery. We still have to sign a great deal of paperwork for the business, order all the supplies for your daily operations, and meet your neighbor."

At the precise moment Artikoa finishes speaking, there's a friendly knock on the door.

"Who could that be?" I hiss with worry.

Artikoa growls softly. "I suggest you answer the door. Keep in mind, I'm not permitted to speak to humans."

Tugging at my sweatshirt, hand painted with my father's jolly face, I rush toward the door and tug it open. Before I can speak—

"Hiya! I'm Betty, your almost roommate. You know, I sure was excited to hear about you moving to town. You're gonna love it in Silver Shoals. If you need someone to show you around, I'm your gal."

I can't keep my jaw from dropping. Betty is the first human I've ever met. Her dark-brown hair is cut sharply at the jawline, and her huge brown eyes beam with happiness. She is more beautiful and friendlier than I ever dreamed.

"I'm Cindy. What's a roommate?"

A low growl emanates from behind me, and before I can correct my blunder, Betty crouches. "Oh my gosh! That's the cutest pupper I've ever seen, dontcha know. What's his name?"

Having no idea what a pupper is, I do my best to act human. "Oh, that's Artikoa. He's my father's most—"

The fox nips at my sweatpants, and I snap my mouth closed. Oh, reindeer poop! There's so much I don't know about this world. I have to keep my true identity a secret! Talking to animals or mentioning my father happens to be Santa will hardly be appropriate. Maybe this Betty person is exactly the friend I need right now.

"Does he bite?"

Bending toward the arctic elder, I mimic Betty's playful tone. "You wouldn't bite my new friend, would you, Arti?"

Growl.

This might be more fun than I'd imagined.

Betty reaches out and strokes Artikoa's fur. "Oh, for goodness' sake! It's even softer than it looks. What a treasure. What are you going to do in the old bakery?"

"What do you mean?"

Betty stands and rubs her hands together. "Downstairs. The retail spot you're renting. Connie Schmenkel used to run a bakery in that there location, but she passed — God rest her — last Christmas. The space has been sitting empty ever since, and my landlord threatened to raise my rent. You came in the nick of time. It's like a Christmas miracle . . . but before Christmas."

Wow. Betty speaks very fast. If everyone in the human world talks like this, I'll have to learn to pay better attention. "You're telling me there already was a bakery here?"

"Oh, you betcha. Best one this side of Pin Cherry Harbor. That's way down south, but reputations and all. I'm sure whatever you do will be a big hit up here. Need help unpacking?" She steps past me and walks toward my stack of luggage.

"No, thank you. I'd actually like to go take a look at the bakery."

Betty turns on the heel of her fuzzy slippers and crinkles up her nose. "You mean you rented this place without looking at it first? That's an odd duck."

Shoot. I did it again. "I — I am so excited to get started. If it was already a bakery, what could go wrong?"

Betty claps her hands together sharply. "I knew it! The second I walked in here, and I smelled peppermint, you know. I knew you were a baker."

"You did?" At least I stop myself from saying how amazing that is, since I don't even know if I'm a baker. I love baking. I enjoyed my after-school job with Cinnamon Roll, but I'm not sure I'll be able to do it on my own.

Betty smacks me hard on the back. "Boy, oh boy. You and I are going to be fast friends. I feel like we already get along like a house on fire." With that, she exits the apartment.

Closing the door and leaning against the thick wood, I struggle to catch my breath. "She thinks I plan on burning this house down?"

Artikoa snickers in his irritating canine way. "One thing you must learn about humans is that they enjoy a variety of verbal shenanigans. Metaphors, similes, aphorisms, exaggerations, puns, and the list goes on. I shall endeavor to help you to the best of my abilities. However, for a girl who speaks every known language on this planet, I would expect you'd have a better understanding of all of this."

"I can tell you right now, Artikoa, book knowledge, or whatever you call it, is nothing compared to landing in the middle of this." I spread my arms wide.

He points his nose to a series of three small hooks beside the door. "The keys to your bakery are there on the red keychain."

"Keys?"

"Unfortunately, here in the human world, most

people lock their doors when they are not present. The doors to their businesses and the doors to their homes. One thing you will quickly learn about humans is they are not all good. The folks who land on your father's Naughty List are there for a reason."

"Betty seems nice."

Artikoa's ears perk and he narrows his gaze. "Are you saying she's on the Nice List?"

"No. I don't know. Am I? Now that I think about it, the moment I laid eyes on Betty, I thought, 'Nice'. I'm not sure, though. I've never had those inklings before."

The fox remains silent, so I change the subject. "Wanna see the bakery?"

"You must learn to use those keys. For this apartment and for your bakery."

Reaching toward the shiny silver keys, I lift them from a small hook and hold them in my palm as though they possess so much promise — actually, they do. These keys hold the promise of my future. Maybe even finding my passion. Everything I hope this independence will bring me. "Let's check it out."

We hurry down the staircase, turn across the landing, and take the second flight of stairs to a small foyer between the bakery and a yarn shop.

Artikoa whispers, "You push the key into that slot and turn it."

Following his instructions, I unlock the door and step into the abandoned bakery.

My bakery.

As I gaze over the empty window displays, pastry case, and the commercial kitchen beyond, my heart swells. I can already see everything! "I'll have displays of all the cookies, cinnamon rolls, tartlets — everything. One of each in the window. Then, I'll organize the pastry case in rows of color. Everything will be green and red and white—"

Artikoa remains motionless by the door.

"Look! There are already baskets on this wall for the fresh bread. I can't wait!"

"Then I suggest we head back upstairs and—"

Betty walks past the fox. "I thought I heard voices down here. Who were you talking to?"

Oops. "Just talking to myself. I'm so excited about getting everything set up. Which elf runs your favorite general store?"

Once again, Betty crinkles up her nose. "Elf? Oh, you're a hoot! An absolute hoot! You should get unpacked. I'll take you over to the Piggly Wiggly tomorrow and help you get your business account set up. You can pay extra for delivery, or you can load up your car and bring everything back here. Pick up will probably save you about $25."

I nod woodenly.

"I'm off to my hot yoga class. Would you like to come over to my place for a glass of wine tomorrow night? After you get settled in?"

"What's— Sure."

As soon as she leaves, I drop to my knees in front of Artikoa. "I didn't understand a word of that. In any language. Help."

I don't appreciate the smug look on his face, but who can blame him?

"There are no elves in the human world, Cynthia. At least not to the human's knowledge. All the businesses in town are run by humans. And everything you desire must be paid for with the currency of the realm."

"Currency?"

"Money. That small chest your mother provided should have enough currency to keep you going until your business turns a profit. You have to pay for things here. It's not like the North Pole."

"So when she mentioned $25 . . . Dollars is their money?"

"Of course. Dollars, euros, pounds Sterling . . . Again, you get the idea. You've learned all these words from books. Now you will learn how they work in real life."

My head spins, and I worry I've made a terrible mistake. "What if I can't do it, Arti? What if—?"

"I was against this idea from the start, Cynthia. For some reason, your father believes in you. If you aren't able to match his faith, perhaps you should return to the North Pole before things go any further with your neighbor."

A little fire begins to flicker in my heart. "No. I can do this. I'm responsible for planning the fastest route ever taken by my father and his reindeer on Christmas Eve. I'm up to the challenge."

Getting to my feet, I brush the dust from my knees and inhale deeply. "I'm going to stay, and I'm going to go to Betty's house tomorrow night and have something called *wine*."

Artikoa seems to snicker as he pads up the stairs without a backward glance.

CHAPTER 5

*B*etty actually made an excellent suggestion. I need to unpack and make this little apartment feel like home.

First things first. I open the small wooden chest to confirm Artikoa's statement. The chest is stuffed with small green-and-white pieces of paper. This must be money. How fun! Grabbing one of the papers, I begin folding and creasing the paper a multitude of times. Eventually, I'm able to create a fairly good likeness of a reindeer.

"Artikoa, look! I made a reindeer."

The fox lifts his eyelids to reveal a mere slit of his mischievous amber eyes. "Money is not a toy, Cindy. Money is used to pay for goods and services in the world of humans. What you've done is created a $20 reindeer. I think you will find that piece of paper will serve you far better tomorrow at the general store — or, as they call it here, a grocery store."

"You don't have to be such a party pooper. I forgot I have to pay for things here." Carefully unfolding the creation, I smooth the paper and place it back in the chest.

Before I can put away my clothes, I have to put up a few strands of twinkling lights, twist a rope of tinsel around the floor lamp, and hang my favorite ornaments from the plain chandelier above the table.

"That's much better. I'll get a tree as soon as the bakery is set up."

Artikoa makes no comment.

Next, I remove all the clothing from my suitcase and fill the drawers in the three-drawer dresser opposite the foot of my bed. By the time I get to the trunk, I'm hungry. "Where do we get food?"

At the mention of food, the fox takes more than a passing interest. "In Silver Shoals, you can find food either in the grocery store or a variety of small restaurants and cafés. Once again, you must pay for your food. I think you'll find I'm not allowed in many of the establishments here."

"That's silly. Where will you eat?"

He walks to the window, lifts his front paws to the sill, and gazes up and down the street. "I wouldn't mind a hunting trip or two, but if we are to maintain our cover, I must be forced to play pet to your human. You will have to buy me a bowl and a water dish." He makes a sound that I've only heard twice in my life. First, when I made a bet with Tassel about how many gingerbread cookies I could eat in one minute, and the second time was when I guzzled an eggnog milkshake that didn't agree with me.

Artikoa composes himself. "I fear I must be domesticated for this assignment."

Joining him at the window, I glance up and down the street and see the rosy glow of a café sign directly opposite my apartment. "I'll run over there and see what they have. Can I bring you something?"

He pushes away from the window and mutters under his breath. "I wouldn't say no to a pair of barely coddled eggs."

"You got it." As I head for the door, my helpful guide offers a reminder. "You will need money, and you must get in the habit of taking your keys to lock the door behind you."

"But you'll be here."

"If the humans are to believe I am your pet—" once again he gags "—you must act as though it were true. In this place, pets are not left in unsecured homes."

"Okay." I grab a few papers from the chest of currency and take the keys from the hook. Closing the door behind me, I fiddle with the lock and struggle to figure out how to secure the door.

A voice echoes through the wood. "Remember, you are human."

A soft chuckle escapes my lips as I jog down the stairs and exit the building.

Halfway to my destination, a screeching sound from my right draws my attention, followed by a blasting honk.

Stopping in the middle of the road, I look toward the sound. That's a real live car. As I walk toward it, I reach out and touch the shiny metal.

The driver inside seems to shake his hand in my direction, so I return the wave.

Next, the window on the side of the car opens, and the person shouts. "Get out of the road, you Santa-loving freak!"

I gasp and grab my sweatshirt as I run toward the café.

That man sounded angry. He said "Santa-loving" like it's a bad thing.

Shrugging my shoulders, I pull open the door and step inside the café. A swirl of intriguing aromas surrounds me.

"Hi, welcome to Sherman's. Table for one?"

"Oh, hi. I don't actually want to buy a table. I was hoping to get some food. You have food here, right?"

The girl tilts her head and scrunches up her nose in an expression that I'm learning to recognize as *I've made another mistake*.

"I do want a table. Sorry. I don't know what I was thinking."

Her mouth smiles. The rest of her face still looks the way Cinnamon Roll and I used to look when Wacky Winkle would come into the bakery and order a pound of acorns. Which we did not carry.

The pleasant woman beckons me to follow her and gestures toward an empty table. I sit down, and she hands me a large plastic book. There's a list of items on one side and numbers on the other. These must be things that they have at this café, and based on what I'm learning about the human world, these numbers must have something to do with money.

"Would you like something to drink?"

"Do you have peppermint hot chocolate?"

Before her face can complete its scrunch, I quickly change my order. "I'll have this." My finger taps the plastic. "Coffee."

The girl exhales as she walks away.

The list of items they have at this café is impressive. And the descriptions make each thing sound super tasty. I want to try everything!

I can hear my mother's voice in my head. "You live right across the street, Marshmallow. There will be plenty of time for you to sample the rest of these items. Just pick one for today."

When the girl returns with my coffee, I smile and try to sound human. "Thank you. I would like to try the vegetable pot pie. And also, I'd like two lightly coddled eggs. But the eggs are not for me. Not here." Shoot. Certainly didn't pull that off.

The girl scratches some words on the notepad in her hand and tilts her head. "I don't think we have coddled eggs. What is that?"

"Oh, it's eggs, like from a tern or a puffin, and then you crack them into a ramekin and put that in boiling water to cook, but not cooking them too much. They still should be pretty runny."

The girl laughs outright. "I know what eggs are. Chicken eggs. I just never heard anyone ask for them coddled. Do you maybe mean poached?"

"Okay. That's right." Wow! I have no idea what I'm getting myself into. I'm pretty sure poached isn't the same as coddled, but hopefully, Artikoa will forgive me.

The girl turns and mumbles under her breath. "Definitely not from around here."

I have to work harder at fitting in.

Eventually, she returns with my pot pie. The crust on top is a lovely golden brown, and as she places it in front of me, delicious aromas of potato, carrot, and turnip reach my nostrils.

"Those super-soft poached eggs — you want those to go, right?"

I don't want the eggs to go anywhere, but somehow, it seems wrong to say that, so I simply nod and hope for the best.

As I finish my pot pie, she returns with a small paper sack. "Are you ready for your bill?"

Without thinking, I reach into my pocket and pull out the pieces of green-and-white paper I took from the chest and hand them to her. "Here's some money."

The not-elf looks at what I've handed her, thumbs through it, and shakes her head. "Oh no. This is too much. I don't know what the exchange rate is in your country, but this is $100. What you ordered is, like, fifteen bucks." She hands several of the pieces of paper back to me and keeps one. "Do you need change, or did you want to leave a tip?"

Once again, I will have to talk to Artikoa about these words. "I don't need anything else. I'm all set."

This time, she rolls her eyes right in front of me before walking back to the kitchen.

My first day in the human world has been exhausting. Finishing the rest of my coffee, I grab the small paper sack and look up and down the street before I cross to my apartment.

Artikoa is pleased with the eggs and tells me they topped the treat with real butter. Which I fail to understand.

"Like the butter we have at the North Pole?"

"No, this butter is made from cow's milk. You'll find reindeer milk scarce in the human world. You'll need to make adjustments to your recipes."

Oh dear, I hadn't thought about that. I wonder what other North Pole ingredients will be unavailable in Silver Shoals.

Tomorrow promises to be ten times the adventure I'd ever imagined.

Artikoa has officially claimed one of the soft green-velvet chairs as his, so I pull an extra blanket from my trunk and throw it across the bed. As I crawl under the covers, a pang of longing touches my heart. I miss Mama and Papa. I miss lively family suppers and hot chocolate before bed. Living on my own will be a big adjustment. Bigger than I'd ever imagined.

Somehow, that tiny flicker in my heart is growing. I'm finding my own way, and maybe, just maybe, baking will be my true passion.

CHAPTER 6

$\mathcal{T}$oday is set-up day. Artikoa and I will get all the paperwork completed. Betty said she'd help me at the grocery store, and I'm going to clean the bakery top to bottom.

Thing is, there's a happy little knock-knock, kn-kn-knock, knock-knock at the door before I even get out of bed.

The rhythm reminds me of one of my papa's silly tunes. "Was that 'Shave and a Haircut, two bits'?"

Artikoa squints with irritation as he whispers, "Ask who it is."

Exhaling loudly, I slap my hands onto the quilt and call out, "Who is it?"

"It's me, dontcha know. I promised to take you

over to the Piggly Wiggly. And I s'pose you haven't got any coffee, so I brought you a cup."

"I was hoping for peppermint hot chocolate," I mumble.

"Beggars can't be choosers." Artikoa closes his eyes and refuses to explain his little comment.

I slept in my sweatshirt and sweatpants, so I shove my feet into slippers and answer the door.

"Good morning, Betty. Thank you for the coffee."

"Oh my gosh! I had no idea you were such a lazybones. You're not even dressed. I'll head back to my place and throw my laundry in a basket. We can stop by the laundromat on our way to the store."

Without further explanation, Betty returns to her apartment.

Closing my door, I mouth the word *laundromat* at Artikoa.

"It's a place where humans wash their clothes. Here in the human world, no elves will be cleaning up after you and laundering your clothing. You'll have to wash it, dry it, and fold it all by yourself."

Icicles! The price of independence is going up every day.

Rummaging through my dresser drawers, I find a pair of red-and-green-striped tights and an oversized sweatshirt/dress with a Christmas tree on the front.

After washing my face and carefully braiding my straight, red hair into two perfect plaits, I get dressed and finish my coffee.

"You should wash that mug before you return it." Artikoa leaps off the cozy green chair and opens the cupboard door under the sink with his teeth.

In the North Pole, we have natural soap flakes for cleaning plates and pots. There's nothing like that in this small cupboard.

Grabbing an old bottle of something called dishwashing liquid, I fill the mug with thick green liquid and try to scrub. Suds almost instantly fill the sink and beyond.

When Betty knocks at the door, it's all I can do to shout, "Come in," over the swell of bubbles floating through the room.

"Oh my goodness! What are you doing over there?" She quickly approaches.

"I wanted to wash up the mug before I gave it back to you."

"You used enough soap to do all the dishes in Silver Shoals for two months!" She glances at the bottle on the counter. "That's a concentrate. You have to use way less than you're used to. Start small. You can always add more, you know."

"Thank you. I just keep messing up." Without warning, tears spring to my eyes.

Betty wraps me in a hug. "Oh, don't cry." She pats my back as I sniffle and swipe at my tears.

"Sorry. It's the first time I've been on my own in a hundred and fifteen years!"

Artikoa growls.

"Oh, you're such a kidder. Look at you. You couldn't be a day over twenty-five if you tried."

As I open my mouth to explain the details of my age, Artikoa runs into the kitchen and jumps on Betty.

I've never seen him behave in such a way.

Betty is unfazed. "Oh, look at this adorable little fur ball. You and I are going to be best buddies, Arti. You're just the sweetest little pupper."

Artikoa, pleased with his diversionary tactic, jogs away.

Betty turns to me. "You have to tell me where you got that dog. I've never seen the breed before. Cutest thing ever. And speaking of adorable, that outfit is to die for."

I have to swallow my objection to dying for clothing. I might actually be starting to get the hang of these human expressions Artikoa mentioned.

"I'm ready to go to the Wiggling Pig. Lead the way."

She presses a hand to her chest and leans over as a fit of laughter grips her. "Goodness me. It's Piggly Wiggly. But I will be calling it the Wiggling Pig from now on!"

As I leave the apartment, Artikoa yips once.

Right. Keys. I grab them off the hook by the door and make a show of locking my apartment.

When we get to the bottom of the two flights of stairs, Betty gestures for me to step outside first.

"I'll lock the door behind us. My shop is usually closed on Thursdays, since I'm open all weekend. So, there shouldn't be any traffic. But better safe than sorry."

That is something I need to take to heart. I've been safe by default my whole life. Worrying about not being safe is a brand-new anxiety.

"This is me, right here." Betty points to a tiny white truck with massive tires.

My first ride in a car! I'll definitely have to hide my excitement.

Betty hops in and takes another key from her key ring, places it in the slot behind the steering wheel, and the car roars to life.

"Fasten your seatbelt!" She giggles and buckles a strap across her chest and lap. I mimic her actions.

"How fun. Why do you have such big tires?"

She sighs. "Technically, it's not my truck. It belongs to my ex-boyfriend. But he said I could use it if I needed. And we need it. Right?"

I want to ask all sorts of questions about ex-boyfriends and trucks. I've read plenty of books about relationships, but I'm still curious what it's like to have a boyfriend in the human world. Maybe there's a way—

"What's your ex-boyfriend's name?"

Betty covers her mouth with one hand and widens her eyes. "What would I like to call him? A lady doesn't talk like that!" A fit of laughter grips her, and she swerves for a moment. "Actually, his name is Sherman. He owns that café across from us. We just broke up last month. 'Cuz he was stepping out on me."

I'll definitely have to ask Arti about that phrase when we get home. "Oh, I had supper there last night. Should I not?"

She reaches across the truck and pats my leg. "You eat wherever you like. No skin off my nose."

Curling elf boots! I should write these down. Betty is practically a walking encyclopedia of metaphors, or whatever Artikoa was talking about.

"I'm sorry to hear that. Are you sure you should be using his truck?"

"What he doesn't know won't hurt him." With that, she squeals so loud my ears ring, and then the car slams to a halt.

"That car in front of me just stopped so suddenly. Sorry, Cindy. I'm a great driver. Honestly."

I have no frame of reference, and the car I saw last night pulled a similar maneuver. Maybe it's all part of driving a car. Tugging at the seatbelt, now tight over my chest, I adjust myself in the seat as she parks in front of the mysterious laundromat.

"You can wait in the car. I'll be quick as a wink."

At least a hundred winks later, Betty returns.

"The grocery store is up around the corner. Like I said, you could walk. But then you'd have to carry everything home. No thanks, I say." She snickers as she makes a turn and gestures to the sign. "Here we are! The Wiggling Pig."

Following her into the Piggly Wiggly, my eyes nearly pop out of my head. The lighting is harsh and I have to squint. There are rows and rows of food in packages. I've never seen anything like it.

"Come on, Cindy. I'll introduce you to the owner and get your account set up. Then we can get you some groceries."

"Sure. Thanks." Scarcely able to put one foot in front of the other, I stumble forward as Betty leads the way through an aisle brimming with boxes claiming to be filled with healthy breakfast cereals. Fruity Puffs! Looks disgusting. Most of the boxes in the row seem rather revolting. I'll take a chewy gingerbread cookie any day.

Betty stops outside a pair of silver double doors and presses a little service button to the left.

A portly man with no hair on the top of his head and a mustache almost as large as my father's, but brown, pushes through the doors with a smile. "Good morning, Betty! And who is your festive friend?"

My lips part, but Betty beats me to the answer. "Oh, this is Cindy, my new neighbor. She just moved into the apartment above the bakery. She's going to reopen Connie Schmenkel's bakery! Isn't that fantastic? She needs to set up a business account and order supplies. My landlord said she paid a year's rent in advance, so she's good for it, Mitch." Betty points to one eye and gives him the biggest wink I've ever seen.

How is it that Betty knows more about my living arrangements than me?

Mitch extends his hand. "Mitch Donaldson. A pleasure to meet you, Cindy. Come on back to my office and we'll get your account set up right now. So happy to have a new business owner in town. People say that Silver Shoals has seen its best days, but I refuse to believe that. We have one of the most magnificent locations on that great lake out there, and there's more to do here than in half the towns around us for miles. That bakery of yours is going to be a smash success. I just know it."

Eventually, he pulls his hand back — I'm not sure what it was for — and we enter his office. He offers Betty and me chairs on the opposite side of his desk.

"Well, it's a real simple form, and for the first three months we bill you weekly. And we don't allow any additional charges until you've taken care of your bill. Does that sound acceptable, Cindy?"

Having learned last night that a bill is something you pay and not a person, I nod my head in agreement.

"Wonderful. Let's get started." Mitch selects a pen from a large cup filled with them on his desk, licks the tip, and smiles. "Let's start with your name?"

"Cynthia Claus. But I prefer Cindy."

Mitch leans back in his chair and taps one end of his pen on his lips as he exchanges a concerned gaze with Betty.

At that moment, I get a brief twitch in my tummy regarding Mitch. Naughty last year, but Nice this year. Oh boy! I must have my dad's gift for the list. I have to tell Artikoa as soon as we get home.

"Your last name is Claus, like Santa?" Mitch laughs uproariously, and Betty joins in.

I fail to get the joke, but quickly join the chuckling.

Mitch begins to write on the form and stops. "I wonder if you're related? That would be something else, wouldn't it?"

Betty, who still hasn't caught her breath from the previous joke, waves away this additional quip.

Struggling to keep my mouth shut, I continue smiling. Clearly, the truth would not be appropriate in this situation.

"Well, I know your address, because Betty said you took the place above the bakery. Now, like I told you, we bill you every week and you can pay by cash or check. We don't take credit cards — usually." He presses a hand to the side of his mouth and leans toward me conspiratorially. "But if you need to pay by card, you just come straight to me. I make exceptions for any friend of Betty's."

"Thank you, Mitch." I have no idea what a "card" is. I'm sure it's not a Christmas card. If those were currency here, then my mother wouldn't have given me the chest of green-and-white paper.

He pauses and looks up. "Do you have your banking information with you? I usually just enter the routing number and account number as a backup. You know, for an emergency."

Having no idea what Mitch is referring to, I

shake my head. "Not yet. We're taking care of all that over the next few days."

Concern furrows his brow for a moment, but he glances at Betty, and she waves his worries away. "She just got into town yesterday, Mitch. Go easy on the gal. Like I said, she's here for at least a year."

They exchange friendly nods, and he makes a note in that section of the form. Then he spins the form around, pushes it toward me, and points to his cup of pens. "Pick your poison, Miss Claus. I need your John Hancock here at the bottom."

Melting snowballs! I don't want poison of any kind, and I have no idea what a John Hancock is.

Betty notices my hesitation and hands me a pen. "You sign your name right here, Cindy. I'm sure you must be overwhelmed with all of this."

"Oh, thank you." Taking the pen, I set about scribing my signature onto the form.

As I get to the "C" in Claus, Betty and Mitch are both leaning toward the paper.

"I've never seen anything like it in my life, Betty. Where would someone even learn that?"

Betty presses her hand to her chest and slowly shakes her head. "It's absolutely beautiful, Cindy. I don't quite know how you're getting gold and red ink to come out of that black ink pen?" She squeaks nervously.

Cookie crumbs! I've always signed my name this way, and of course, no one in the North Pole gave it a second thought. Elves have some of the finest penmanship in the world. My mother is a master calligrapher. As for changing the color of the ink . . . I'm still learning how to manage my half-elven, one-quarter angel powers.

"It's a silly party trick. See?" I hold the pen out for both of them to look at. "I swapped pens." My magic has changed the plastic instrument into a gold filigree writing tool with burnished scrollwork all around. They both gasp and exchange an unreadable glance.

"It's more fun if I don't warn you. It is my actual signature, though. So that's okay, right?"

Mitch cautiously pulls the form back across his desk and nods once. "That'll do. Will you ladies be shopping today?"

"Yes. I need to get some ingredients for my recipes. And for peppermint hot chocolate."

Mitch mumbles. "Really committed to this Christmas thing, aren't you?"

"Oh, I really am. You can keep the pen."

At that, his face brightens, and he accepts the beautiful writing instrument.

Betty grabs my hand and tugs me from the office. "Cindy, I don't want to tell you how to live your life, but people in Silver Shoals are kind of old-fashioned. Some might even call them boring. Party tricks like that are likely to make folks suspicious. Maybe just keep them for special occasions, not for signing forms at the Wiggling Pig." Her attempt to add a dash of humor at the end does not go unnoticed.

"Sorry about that. I can't tell you how much I appreciate all your help, Betty. You're a true friend."

"Oh! Now you're gonna make me cry." She dabs at her eyes, but she's smiling.

I'm going to interpret those as imaginary happy tears and continue with this shopping adventure.

CHAPTER 7

*A*fter extensive debate, Betty and I decide it will be best to stick to personal groceries today. It doesn't make much sense to load the bakery with supplies and then have to move them back and forth all day while I clean.

At the register, Betty tells me to put them on my account, but the account was for my business, and that doesn't seem like the honest thing to do.

I don't argue with her, but I hand some of the green-and-white papers to the lady wearing the red Piggly Wiggly shirt. She takes the money and gives me a receipt and change.

This is my first time seeing coins in this currency, and I have to admit I'm fascinated. Betty grabs three of my bags and clucks her tongue. "Come on, Cindy. You grab the rest of the bags, and we'll swing by the laundromat on the way home."

"Oh, right."

At the laundromat, I follow Betty inside. I watch as she moves clothing from the washing machine to the dryer, and inserts coins. Fantastic! I'll be able to use these coins on a future project. How fun!

Betty sets my grocery bags outside my door and asks if I want to come over for supper or just wine.

"Hmmm. I'll eat at home tonight, and then we'll have wine after. Is that okay?"

She shrugs her shoulders and smiles. "Any way you slice it. I'll see you later for a glass of Pinot."

"Okay."

Dragging my bags inside, I close the door and can't hide my smile when Artikoa asks for details.

"It was amazing! I've never seen so much food in all my life. I didn't get anything for the bakery yet. I thought it would be best to clean first."

At the mention of food, he hops down from his cozy perch and noses through grocery bags. "What did you get me?"

"Well, eggs. I know you love those. And then

Betty told me to try chicken. I don't plan on eating it, but I'll make it for you if you'd like."

He sniffs the air, and a shrug ripples across his back. "I prefer mine fresher, but I suppose we're all making sacrifices."

"By the way, Betty said the bakery has been empty for nearly a year. Her ex-boyfriend Sherman was determined to relocate his café to our side of the street. The bakery and Betty's shop combined are about half again the size of his current location."

Artikoa paces near the bags. "And now?"

"Now that I've moved in, he's considering acquiring Betty's store as a prep kitchen, which would allow him to shrink the size of his current kitchen and expand the seating. However, Betty informed me she's no longer interested in subletting to Sherman. Since I'm paying rent on the bakery and this apartment, the landlord has ceased his threats regarding a rent increase."

The fox nods thoughtfully. "The bakery is in great shape. The equipment and most of the pans and utensils have been left in place. Why don't you toss a piece of that chicken in a bowl before you head downstairs?"

"You got it!" The chicken is slimy and cold. Two textures I don't enjoy. I place a piece in a bowl, set it on the floor, and wash my hands like crazy!

"Come on down and join me if you get lonely."

There's a sharp scoff behind me as I close the door — but I don't lock it.

I have a small notepad on the counter for making a list of things I'll need. Making a list causes me to think of Papa. He loves making lists and checking them over a couple of times.

As I scrub dust from the front window, it dawns on me that I'll need a sign. Many of the shops along the narrow street have wooden signs hanging perpendicular to the sidewalk, as well as painted signs in their windows. I'm certain Betty knows the person who does the sign painting, but I'm going to send a letter to my father and see if the elves would have time to make my wooden sign. It would certainly make me feel good to have a reminder of home.

Flipping to a blank sheet in my notepad, I write a quick note. I've never actually written a letter to Santa before, but I know they always arrive. The elves who work in the mailroom sort through stacks of letters every year.

I'll have to run to the post office for an envelope and a stamp tomorrow, but I'm sure Papa will be happy to hear from me.

With that out of the way, I continue cleaning

and organizing. As I'm gathering up the cleaning supplies and my notepad, hoping to return to my apartment, there's a knock on the window.

When I glance toward the street, there's a man in a bright-red stocking cap waving at me through the glass.

"Hi!" I wave and walk toward the window. "We're not open."

He points to his ear and shakes his head.

I point toward the door, and we meet on the stoop. After unlocking the door, I open it and try to explain.

The man waves away my explanation. "I'm Ronnie Schmenkel, the landlord. My wife used to run a bakery out of this place. I saw the lights on and thought maybe Sherman was setting up shop over here after all. The paperwork for the year lease went through so quick . . . Never met the guy in person. Are you the new renter?"

"I am. My name's Cindy."

Ronnie shoves a hand at me, and once again, I'm puzzled by this ritual. However, I'm learning that mimicry is my best defense. So I shove a hand right back. He grabs my hand and shakes it vigorously. Wow. That's new.

"Nice to meet you, Cindy. What kind of business do you plan on running out of this place?"

"I'm setting up a bakery. I plan on specializing in Christmas treats year around. Of course, I'll have other things too, like bread and muffins."

Ronnie takes a ragged breath and seems suddenly choked with emotion. "Well, that must be warming my Connie's heart up in heaven. Nothing would make her happier than to know her passion for baking will live on."

"Thank you. I love baking. Here's hoping it might be my passion, too."

"I've got a couple of her old recipe books at home. They're not doing me any good. I'll bring them by tomorrow if you'd like."

Nice. Ronnie is definitely on the Nice List. That time, I got the tingling and a sense of certainty. "I'd love that. Thank you."

"Connie loved Christmas baking." His voice catches in his throat, and he nods silently as he backs away. He manages to choke out, "Tomorrow" before he disappears down the street.

Daylight hours last longer here than at the North Pole, but the sun has already set, and Artikoa will expect his supper.

Locking the bakery, I spin the key ring around my finger as I walk up to the apartment. This independence thing is going to work. Today was a difficult day, but I enjoyed every part. People have been so kind. I had no idea Silver Shoals would be the perfect location when I chose it, but it seems like it is.

"You ready for some supper?"

"That would be lovely, Cynthia. How was your time in the bakery?"

Artikoa and I catch up over our meal, and when I remind him of my plans to have a glass of wine with Betty, he once again snickers.

"Is there something I should know about this wine?"

"It's probably better if you figure it out on your own. This is all about independence, isn't it?" He turns, hops onto his favorite chair, and closes his eyes.

Fine. I'll figure it out on my own. I'm doing a great job by myself, and there's no reason to quit now.

Whipping up a small batch of gingerbread cookies, I fill a plate and head across the hall. I don't take my keys or lock the door. Artikoa must be sleeping soundly, or he's given up on reminding me, because he makes no sound as I close the door behind me.

"Welcome!" Betty steps back as she invites me into her apartment.

While my color scheme is mostly green, white, and red, Betty's is like a rainbow. Everything is brightly colored, and there are hand-knitted and crocheted items everywhere. Even a gorgeous hand-crocheted blue-purple-and-teal hanging lampshade!

"Did you make all these things?"

"I did. I have a mild obsession with yarn."

"Everything is beautiful. You're so talented!"

"Thank you. Let me take those cookies." She places the green plate of cookies on a low table in front of her sofa and fills two tall, stemmed glasses with a deep-red liquid.

"I'm not sure if gingerbread goes with Pinot, but we're about to find out." She lifts her glass to continue, but I respond without thinking.

"Cookies go with everything."

Betty chuckles. "Here's to new friends and new beginnings."

She clinks her glass against mine and startles me. Then she drinks.

I follow suit.

Oh boy. This tastes spoiled. I can't spit it out, but I'm not sure I can swallow it either. Struggling to get it down, I'm happy to see that Betty isn't paying attention. I would hate to offend her.

"Isn't it delicious! There such a nice note of tart cherry, and maybe even a little chocolate."

It tastes like no chocolate I've ever had. "Do you drink a lot of wine?"

This question brings a huge chuckle from

Betty. "Doesn't everyone? Some days, I'm not sure how I'd get along without it."

I can certainly think of many things I'd rather have. In fact, maybe I can get this taste out of my mouth with a delicious cookie. Placing my glass on the low table, I grab a cookie.

They don't taste as good as the gingerbread cookies from the North Pole, but Artikoa did warn me how substituting ingredients could bring different flavors.

With each sip of wine, I take a bite of cookie. The gingerbread helps disguise the strange taste of the red liquid, and I manage to work my way through part of the glass.

Betty seems to have no such problem. She's almost finished with her second glass. The more she consumes, the more she talks.

"Like I told you. Sherman Canton was stepping out on me. There's a woman who works at the local library who checks out more than an occasional book. According to the gals at the bingo hall, she's responsible for destroying ten different relationships in town. Apparently, she's great at prying men away from their wives or girlfriends, but then she has no use for them!"

This seems to be gossip. My mother warned me against it at a young age. When I would come home from school or a party and start talking about this elf or that elf, my mother would always say, "And who is here to defend her?" I quickly learned that talking behind someone's back was inappropriate. Apparently, Betty has no problem with it.

"And the man who runs the laundromat! Don't even get me started."

I have no intention of getting her started. The question is how to get her to stop.

"He's got quite a problem with drink, if you know what I mean." She pantomimes tipping a glass of something into her mouth. "The local watering hole, Shallow Shoals, has to kick him out almost nightly! Can you believe it? They refuse to continue serving him, and he makes a scene. Every night!" Betty fans one hand in the air. "Some people."

I definitely don't like this side of Betty. Before she had the wine, she was friendly and helpful. Although, she did make that comment to Mitch about my rent being paid for a year . . . Maybe my first human friend isn't as perfect as I thought.

When Betty starts in with a tale about the mayor taking bribes, I can't take it anymore. "Betty, I have such a big day ahead of me tomorrow. I'm grateful for the wine, but I really should get home."

She glances at my half-full glass and frowns.

"You hardly touched your Pinot, Cindy. Don't tell me you're a teetotaler!" She reaches across the table and pours the rest of my drink into her glass. "Waste not, want not!"

Leaving the plate of cookies behind, I head toward the door. "Thanks again."

CHAPTER 8

ITH NO CHRISTMAS CAROLS to wake me, I hoped I'd be able to sleep in. Apparently, over one hundred years of conditioning is hard to break. My eyes open in relative darkness — nothing new — and I roll out of bed to make some hot chocolate. Sitting at the small kitchen table, I stir my hot chocolate with a candy cane until the air fills with the delicious aroma of peppermint.

I take a careful sip, and the liquid warms my tummy and my heart. "Not as good as home, but it's a start."

Artikoa offers to keep me company in the bakery while I finish making my list.

When we reach the bottom of the stairs,

Ronnie Schmenkel waves brightly through the glass window in the front door.

Icicles! "I forgot the key."

Artikoa chuckles softly.

Waving back, I point to the lock and press a hand to my forehead. Then I race up the steps, grab the keys, lock the apartment, and hurry back down to open the door to the foyer for Ronnie.

"Morning, Cindy. I figured if you're anything like my Connie was, you'd be getting an early start. Here are those recipes I told you about."

In his arms, Ronnie holds two books that appear to be handmade.

"Oh, those look lovely. Come on in to the bakery, and you can set them on the counter."

As I fumble with the lock on the bakery, Ronnie offers encouragement. "You need to wiggle the key up and down a bit, dear. Once you get the hang of it, it'll be no trouble at all."

I give the key a little jiggle, and sure enough, the lock twists right open.

Ronnie places the books on the counter with a low hum of reverence.

"Are you sure you want me to have these? They seem like such a wonderful memento of your wife."

He withdraws his hand and shakes his head. "They're not doing me any good. And I know Connie, God rest her. She'd want to know her recipes were still putting a smile on someone's face."

"Thank you, Ronnie. It's really special to be able to do this for her." Hopefully, that's the right thing to say.

Ronnie nods and gets a faraway look in his eyes.

It's difficult for me to understand what he's feeling. I've never known anyone who's died. Elves seemingly live forever. My father and I were the only ones with even a drop of human blood at the North Pole. My father's angelic heritage gives him abilities we continue to learn about with each passing century. Can't imagine what it would be like to lose someone you love. "I can't wait to make Connie's recipes."

Respectfully opening the book, my heart fills with love when I see careful script on each page. Connie hand-wrote these recipes. Each and every one contains little hearts and sketches in her own hand. She truly loved baking. "These are amazing. I hope I can do these recipes justice."

Ronnie reaches out and pats the book. "Connie always said there was a secret ingredient in every one of her recipes."

Glancing at the hearts on the page, I smile. "Was it love?"

Ronnie sniffles. "You betcha."

"I'm going to try this recipe for rye bread as soon as I get my ingredients in. Should I save a loaf for you?"

Ronnie swipes an errant tear from his wrinkled cheek. "That would be real sweet, you know."

"Thanks again for these recipes. I'll treasure them. Now, I better get busy, or I'll never get this place open."

As the kind gentleman hobbles toward the door, a thought pops into my head. "Hey, do you happen to know who paints the signs in the shop windows?"

"Sure do. That's my cousin Sven Tollesson. My aunt married a Swede, and all the kids got them unusual foreign names. His shop is over behind the laundromat. Sven's Signs. It's in the book."

Ronnie leaves, and I wonder what book he's talking about.

My plan to finish my list and walk to the grocery store takes about an hour longer than intended, but the upside is I pass by the laundromat and take a detour to Sven's.

There's a small wooden sign in the window that says, "open." Turning the handle, I pull the door and step inside. "Hello? Anyone here?" There's a handbell on the counter next to a sign that says ring for service. I lift the bell and ring out the chorus of "Jingle Bells."

The largest man I've ever seen stomps from the back room. "No need to play a whole solo. One ring'll do it."

"I'm so sorry. I love bells. I couldn't help myself."

He takes one look at my green sweatpants and red sweatshirt embroidered with reindeer, and chuckles. "I suppose it is the season and all that. What can I do you for?"

Confusing, but not as confusing as dying for clothing or selecting poison pens. "Your cousin Ronnie told me you paint all the signs in the windows of the businesses on Main Street."

"Ol' Ronnie's doing some marketing for me, eh?"

I'm guessing that means yes, so I continue. "I'm opening a bakery—"

"No way! In Connie's old place?"

"Yes. Ronnie was most kind. He gave me some of Connie's recipes. I can't wait to try them."

Sven strokes his thick blond beard and nods solemnly. "It was real hard on him when Connie passed. It'll do his heart good to know someone's making her recipes again. What are you gonna call the place?"

"Actually, my father came up with the name. Yuletide Me Over Bakery."

Sven slaps the knee of his work pants hard.

"Well, I'll be a monkey's uncle. That's fantastic. Thought maybe you were gonna keep calling it Connie's Confections, but your thing is much better. Folks around here will love it. I've got a pretty light afternoon if you'd like me to come up and get that painted today. What color are you thinking?"

"Maybe red and gold? I'm going to feature Christmas treats year-round, with other stuff. But I'd kinda like to keep the colors festive."

Sven looks me up and down and grins. "I should've known by the sweatshirt, eh?"

At least I don't have my father's face on my shirt today. "I suppose. Folks say I'm a little obsessed with Christmas. Betty thinks it's adorable."

At the mention of my neighbor, Sven's expression turns dark. "You be careful around her. That Betty Troup has a way of stirring up trouble. Her mouth works twice as fast as her conscience. She stirred up a real hornet's nest for me and the missus last year. Bunch of lies! But that didn't stop her."

A chill creeps across my shoulders. "Thanks for letting me know. My mother taught me not to gossip, but I know that's not what everyone learned."

"Ain't that the truth?"

Sven promises to stop by later with a selection of paints and a font book.

"Thank you. See you this afternoon."

Continuing to the Piggly Wiggly, I grab a large cart and crawl down each aisle with the speed of a newborn polar bear.

Everything is so unfamiliar. I'm forced to read every label and second-guess every choice.

By the time I reach the register, the sun is high overhead.

It occurs to me as I load the bags back into the cart that I absolutely cannot carry all of this back to the bakery. "Is it alright if I push the cart home? I'll unload my groceries and bring it right back."

The woman in the checkout lane smiles warmly. "You're that new girl, Cindy, right?"

"Yes. I'm opening a bakery."

"You go ahead and push that cart home and park it in the alley behind your store. Next time you come, just bring it with you for a refill."

"Thank you! That's wonderful." Struggling to swallow, I have to ask, "Alley?"

The woman chuckles and straightens the nametag on her apron. "You probably haven't even had time to step out there. It's mostly for deliveries and the trash pickup. But if you walk out the back door of your bakery, you'll see you've got yourself a little parking spot back there for your car."

"I don't have a car. Should I get one?"

Dottie — that's the name on her tag — laughs

good-naturedly. "That's a decision between you and your checkbook, sweetie."

That's the second time someone has mentioned something about a check. Add it to my list of things to talk to Artikoa about.

Pushing the cart uphill is harder than I'd imagined. I have to stop several times to catch my breath. Although, every time I stop, I get a different view of this special little town and the great lake stretching as far as the eye can see beyond the shoals.

The sky is the blue-grey of winter, free of clouds. The sun illuminates the snow and ice covering the lake, and everything sparkles with newness and excitement.

Eventually, I reach the bakeshop. Rather than trying to park the cart on the sloping sidewalk in front of the bakeshop, I look around until I find a road that leads me to what I'm hoping is an alley.

Pushing the cart, I find the back doors to the bakery and Betty's yarn shop.

Dottie was right. There's a large trash receptacle behind the bakery, and a small parking spot beside it.

I may not have a car, but this is a nice flat area to park the cart while I unload.

As I come out to make the final trip with my

groceries, Betty is standing on her back step smoking a cigarette.

Having only seen them in books, I had no idea how terrible they smelled.

"Good morning, almost-roomy. That was such a fun night, wasn't it?"

With the new knowledge I gained about Betty today, I hesitate to answer.

Her face pinches with concern. "Cindy? Are you feeling okay?" She blows stinky smoke into the air.

"Yes. I'm distracted by all the bakery stuff. What did you say?"

Betty flicks her cigarette to the ground and grinds it out with the toe of her boot. "Oh, doesn't matter. I've got to get the store open. Let me know if you need any help with setup." She opens the door and walks into her yarn shop, leaving the smashed cigarette on the ground.

My eyes wander over the dirty snow beside her steps, and notice several more cigarette butts poking through the crust. Yuck. I'd love to stop and clean them up, but I have to focus on the bakery. If I have time when I'm finished, I'll come back out and clean that up tonight.

Taking the last load of groceries into the bakery, I hum "O Tannenbaum" as I put everything away.

Connie had a wonderful system in the bakery. Things are located exactly where I would've put them if I'd designed the place myself.

"Maybe I'll make a batch of cookies before Sven arrives. Then he can tell me what he thinks. He probably had tons of Connie's cookies."

Scratching at the front door of the bakery distracts me from my baking objective.

"Artikoa, what are you doing?" He looks over his shoulder to be sure there are no humans around and replies, "I can't exactly open round door handles with these paws. The apartment has a lever, but this—"

"Right." I open the door, and in he saunters. "You've cleaned things up nicely, Cynthia. What's left on your list?"

"Sven is coming to paint the sign on the window, but I thought I'd ask Papa if the elves could carve me a wooden sign for outside." Mention of the elves reminds me of my unfinished errands. "Melting snowballs! I need to get that letter to the post office."

Grabbing the folded piece of paper from the counter, I head for the door. "Do you want to come with me?"

Artikoa lolls his head back and forth thoughtfully. "I suppose it wouldn't hurt to get the lay of the land."

The warmth of the sun on my shoulders is brand new. My mother's magic kept everything at a lovely temperature in our North Pole dome, but having the actual sun warm me is a fresh thrill. Based on the happy skip in Artikoa's step, I'd say he feels the same way.

"There's the post office. Do you think I can buy a stamp here?"

Artikoa whispers so softly I can barely hear him. "Remember, you're human, and I have agreed to lower myself to the humble status of domestic canine. We cannot openly chat. But, of course they will sell stamps."

Holding the door open, I gesture for Artikoa to enter. He sits firmly on the step and shakes his head. Only then do I notice the sign on the door: No pets allowed. Service animals only.

No idea what a service animal is, but if Artikoa is pretending to be a pet, then he's definitely not allowed.

There are two people in line with packages.

When it's my turn at the window, I smile brightly at the worker and ask, "May I have an envelope and a stamp, please?"

"What's the rate of postage?"

"I'm sorry. I don't understand the question."

The worker rolls his eyes. "Where are you sending your letter?"

"The North Pole."

For a moment, the man's jaw hangs slack. "You know somebody up there, do you?" The tone is not friendly, but I choose to ignore that.

"Yes. Thank you. So one envelope and one stamp for the North Pole."

He taps several keys, exhales loudly, and hands me an envelope and three stamps.

"I only need—"

"You said North Pole, right? You'll need all three of those stamps. Now step out of line while you address your envelope."

The man is so angry. I'm not sure what I've done to upset him, but I take the envelope and the stamps and step out of line as he instructed.

I write the address of the bakery in one corner of the envelope, as I've seen on so many of the children's letters addressed to my father. Then I write Santa Claus, North Pole in large letters, on two lines, in the center of the envelope. Placing my letter inside, I seal it and affix the stamps.

There's one person in line, so I patiently wait my turn.

When I pass my envelope to the postman, he laughs out loud. "Aren't you a little old to be writing letters to Santa?"

"Oh, he's my— It's for a child."

That's the closest I've ever come to lying in my

entire life. Technically, in elf years, I am a child. This angry man doesn't need to know that.

"Whatever you say." He tosses the envelope in a large plastic bin and looks straight through me. "Next."

CHAPTER 9

s we stroll back to the bakery, three separate people stop me on the sidewalk to tell me how adorable my dog is and ask if they can pet him. Each time Artikoa growls, but endures the attention. One asks if he's a rescue. After they leave, I get the scoop on that term from the fox.

We decide that if we're leaning into this "dog" thing, we might as well add the rescue detail to his story. Since Arti is an enchanted fox, he's technically been rescued from the mortal woes of an actual Arctic beast. Seems like being a human involves more stretching of the truth than I'd imagined.

My feelings still sting from the postal worker's comments. It doesn't make any sense, but I can't seem to let it go. After a certain age, humans refuse to believe in the existence of my father. Snowflakes! It's not my job to fix that. I have cookies to bake.

Placing Connie's handcrafted cookbook on the metal worktable in the bakery kitchen, I lay both hands on the padded gingham cover and close my eyes.

"Connie Schmenkel, thank you for creating these amazing recipes. I promise to honor your memory each time I bake. Guide me and help me add love to every recipe. Let's bake!"

A subtle chill wafts over my skin. Rubbing my arms, I click the oven on to preheat and turn to the first recipe I want to test.

Once I'm in baking mode, my spirits soar. I'm even singing carols out loud as I measure and mix ingredients.

This gingerbread cookie recipe is different from the ones Cinnamon Roll and I made at the North Pole, and I'm curious to find out if Connie had a better idea.

Despite the heat from the oven, a coolness swirls around me.

"They sure do smell good, don't they?" Inhaling deeply, I await a reply.

Artikoa lifts his nose and sniffs the air. "As you

know, cookies would not be my first choice, but these do have a pleasant aroma."

The timer on the double-door oven pings and I grab my red-and-green oven mitt from the counter.

Cooling the cookies on the tray for five minutes, per Connie's recipe, I can hardly wait to pop one in my mouth.

Eating hot cookies might burn my tongue, but over the years I've built up callouses.

Once the second timer pings, it's time to transfer the cookies to cooling racks, but I freeze with indecision.

Artikoa chuckles from the front of the bakeshop. "Just eat one, Cynthia. You can have another after you ice them."

Now that I have permission—

Picking up the luscious warm cookie, I take a generous bite and savor the delicious combination of molasses and spice. "These are easily as good as the ones from the North Pole!" Rather than a reply, Artikoa yips once.

"What's going on? Did you—"

Sven Tollesson stands in the middle of my bakery with a confused look wrinkling his brow. "You were kidding around about the North Pole, eh?"

Refusing to tell two almost lies in one day, I

simply nod and laugh. Pretending my mouth is too full for an answer.

He places the book and a fan of color swatches on the counter. "First you choose the font, then you can pick from these colors. There are a few different shades of gold, and, well, reds are all over the place."

Swallowing with difficulty, I approach the fonts. Paging through sheet after sheet of perfect letters reminds me of my mother's calligraphy practice book. When I get to the typeface called Christmas Cheer, I nearly cry. "This one! This is perfect."

From his towering height above me, Sven easily gazes over my shoulder. "Good choice. Now, the colors. I was thinking red lettering with a gold outline and maybe a little fancy scrollwork. Would you like that?"

"I would."

He pushes the color swatches closer to me, and I select Filigree for my golden color. As I thumb through the red swatches, my heart nearly stops when I see a color named Santa's Sleigh. "This is perfect. And it's so shiny. Just like the real thing!"

Sven arches one eyebrow as he reads the color name from the swatch book. "If you say so, miss."

Reindeer poop! I did it again. Maybe if I distract him with some baked goods . . . "Sven, would you like a gingerbread cookie?"

The mountain of a man turns slowly toward me. "Gingerbread is my favorite. How did you know, eh?"

"I didn't. I'm trying some of Connie's recipes, and that one caught my eye."

He strokes his thick beard and nods thoughtfully. "I haven't had one of Connie's cookies since—"

Oops. Better press on. "Iced or plain?"

He swallows hard and clears his throat to hide his emotion. "Iced, please. A little extra, if you don't mind."

"I'd never mind. I can't seem to eat gingerbread cookies without extra icing." Chuckling to myself, I walk into the kitchen and pipe thick squiggles of icing on half-a-dozen cookies.

Placing the cookies on a green plate, I return to the front room. "Here you are, sir."

"Thank you, Cindy. What do I owe you?"

"Owe me? Oh, like a bill? No. No. No. My treat. I just love to see people enjoying the things I make."

He holds up a cookie and smiles so wide I can practically see all of his teeth. "You sound just like Connie. You better charge people once in a while, or you'll never be able to keep this roof over your head. Charity starts at home. That's what my sweet mother used to say."

"That's a good thing to remember. Does your mother not say that anymore?"

He stops chewing and stares at me.

"You said she used to say it. I was wondering why she doesn't say that anymore?"

He swallows the bite in his mouth and brushes crumbs from his beard. "My mother passed a couple years before Connie. I'm the youngest of ten children, so she was quite advanced in age by the time I was born."

"Oh. Sorry. You must miss her."

I can't imagine what it would be like to lose my mother. I may have left the North Pole to have some independence, but any time I want to see her, all I have to do is go back. Knowing she's there comforts me.

Sven finishes another cookie and nods. "I know she's looking down on me from heaven. And that warms my heart, you know?"

"I absolutely do. I'll let you get to painting while I finish this batch of cookies. Would you like to take some home?"

The temporary cloud of sadness lifts, and Sven nods enthusiastically. "I sure would. I've got half-a-dozen little Swedish meatballs at home that would gobble those up."

As I return to the kitchen, I take a moment to decipher his comment. Since he comes from such a large family, and Ronnie mentioned that Sven's father was Swedish, I'm guessing the "half-a-dozen Swedish meatballs" he referred to are his children. Look at that. I'm getting the hang of it. Humans aren't that complicated, after all.

When I finish the batch of cookies, I decide to make twelve dozen more and create little gift packages for all my neighbors on Main Street. By the time I put the third batch of gingerbread cookies in the oven, Sven is finished painting.

"Why don't you come and tell me what you think, Cindy?"

After washing the icing from my hands, I step into the retail area and glance at the window. "It's backward!"

Sven belly laughs until he can hardly catch his breath. "Follow me, miss."

He opens the door and leads me out to the sidewalk in front of my shop, then gestures up toward the window.

"Oh! I feel so foolish. Of course, I want people to be able to read it when they're passing by. I suppose that's why it's Sven's Signs and not Cindy's Signs."

This brings another round of raucous laughter.

"Welcome to Silver Shoals, Cindy. I hope your bakery is a huge success."

"Thank you. And I hope you have a Merry Christmas."

AFTER SUPPER, ARTIKOA AND I go over the checklist he asked me to create.

"I've opened an account at the grocery store. I kind of understand the laundromat. Then, there's the discovery of the alley behind the bakeshop. I know that's not on the list, but I thought it was worth mentioning."

"Tomorrow, you'll head to the bank and get your accounts set up. It isn't a great idea to have a chest full of currency in your apartment. You can keep a few bills here for emergencies. But it will be helpful for you to have a checking account. What else is on the list?"

The scream from across the hall shocks us both.

"What was that?"

Artikoa's compact ears point toward our door with sharp tension. "I have no idea. However, that was no squeal of joy. I'm familiar with fear in creatures, and that scream was pure terror. Perhaps we should check on her."

Placing my pen on the table, I rise from the chair and walk toward the door. Before I reach it, Betty's door slams and heavy footsteps race down the stairs.

Pulling open my door, I run to the railing and look over, but all I see is the hood of a sweatshirt pulled forward. I can't see the face. Whoever it is storms out the front door, and it slams behind them as they disappear into the night.

Knocking on Betty's door, I wait, but there's no answer. "Betty? Hey, is everything all right?"

Artikoa pushes up beside me. "I smell blood. You better go in. She could be injured."

Without a thought for myself, I open the door and hurry into Betty's apartment. Laid out under the colored light from her hand-crocheted lampshade — is Betty.

The gold filigree pen I gave Mitch at the grocery store protrudes from her neck.

Swallowing the horror, I hurry to Betty and shake her. "Hey! Betty, open your eyes. You're gonna be fine."

Artikoa steps beside me and nuzzles my shoulder. "She's dead, Cynthia. In the human world, when someone passes away — under circumstances like this — one must call the authorities."

"Call?"

"There's a phone in your apartment. I'll show you."

Sure enough. Having completely escaped my notice earlier, there's a phone on the wall. Artikoa instructs me to dial the digits 911 and tell them what we've discovered.

A helpful man on the other end of the phone takes all the information, confirms our address, and tells me to remain calm.

"Okay. Do you think the person who hurt her will come back?"

He asks if the intruder is still on the premises.

"No. The person ran out. That's when I went to check on Betty. Because of the scream."

The man informs me the deputies will take my statement and secure the crime scene when they arrive. He also tells me not to touch anything.

"What if I already did?"

The wailing sirens interrupt the call, and the man says he's going to hang up and I should tell the deputies everything I told him.

The deputies rush up the stairs, take one look at me, and ask me if I have a weapon.

"A weapon? No. Why would you think that?" As the words come out of my mouth, and I raise my hands, I notice they're covered with Betty's blood.

"Turn and face the wall, miss. Put your hands behind your back."

Doing as I'm told, Artikoa growls and advances on the two men.

"Ma'am, tell your dog to back off. We'll send animal control over to retrieve him later."

Everything is happening so fast. I don't understand any of it.

The second deputy enters Betty's apartment and begins talking into his radio. Calling for things like a "medical examiner" and "backup."

The first deputy propels me down the stairs and puts me into the back of his vehicle.

I hope Artikoa escapes from the apartment. He's very clever. I don't know what an animal control is, but it doesn't sound good.

As the deputy's vehicle pulls away from the curb, the flashing lights on top illuminate the bakery window.

Yuletide Me Over Bakery is closed before it even opened.

CHAPTER 10

*W*hen we arrive at the sheriff's station, the deputy pulls me out of the car and takes me inside. He advises me of a thing called Miranda and tells me I'm charged with the homicide of Betty Troup.

Homicide is murder! How on earth— "I didn't hurt Betty. I was in my apartment when she screamed."

"You've been advised of your rights, miss. You're entitled to have an attorney. Are you sure you want to keep talking without one?"

There is no crime in the North Pole, so very little time was spent on criminal matters during my education.

I know about things like lawyers and police officers, but I never thought I'd find myself in this predicament.

"I didn't do anything wrong. I'm telling the truth."

The deputy nods, but his expression is not one of belief. "You can tell your story to the judge at your arraignment."

He presses my fingers into ink and places the prints on a card. Then he takes two pictures of me, jots down my personal details, and locks me in a cell.

I've been away from the North Pole for a grand total of seventy-two hours, and this is where my wonderful plans for independence have taken me.

I'd give just about anything to hear my mother say, I told you so.

There's a scratchy wool blanket folded on the end of the bench where I'm sitting. If that deputy thinks I'll get one wink of sleep tonight, he's sadly mistaken. Between feeling sorry for myself and worrying about Artikoa, I certainly won't be closing my eyes. With nothing better to do, I'm forced to endure flashes of the night's events.

The scream.

The door slamming.

Thundering footsteps.

The hoodie.

Was it black or dark green?

Whoever ran from Betty's apartment didn't have to stop and unlock the front door.

That means either they had a key, or Betty let them in and didn't lock the door behind them.

As far as I know, Betty and I have the only keys to that front door. If that's true, she must have known—

"Miss Claus, you're free to go."

"What? So you believe what I said?"

The deputy opens the cell and gestures for me to step out. "I'm not here to decide guilt or innocence, miss. But your bail has been posted and you're free to leave. Check with the desk clerk to get your arraignment date and sign for your personal belongings."

My brain searches through snippets of memory to identify the term posting bail as I walk out from the rear of the station.

Towering a foot above all the deputies stands Sven. "You're lucky Ronnie's insomnia was acting up, miss. He was listening to his police scanner when he heard the news about your arrest. And don't worry about your dog. My cousin works at animal control and owed me a favor. That pup of yours should still be safe at the apartment."

"Thank you, Sven. Did you post the bail?"

"It was Ronnie. But his sciatica was acting up,

so he asked me to pick up the money and take care of it."

Sven motions for me to follow him, and as we step outside, the icy wind blowing down Main Street cuts right through my sweatshirt. I shiver until my teeth chatter.

"Take my coat, miss. This wind here is nasty cold some days."

His coat nearly reaches my ankles, but it's as warm and toasty as a cup of cocoa. "Thank you. I guess winter takes some getting used to."

"Didn't it get this cold where you came from?"

"No. Not exactly." I can't possibly let myself head down that road. "Thanks for the coat."

This kind man drives me back to my bakery in his work truck. There's a shifter on the floor. The truck is quite loud. It's difficult to carry on a conversation, but Sven's voice somehow cuts through the noise.

"I never jump to conclusions, miss, but how did you manage to get arrested for Betty's murder?"

Murder. What a terrible word. "It was all a big misunderstanding." After I explain what I heard and what I did, he nods and exhales slowly. "You shouldn't have touched the body. That's the first thing you learn watching these TV detective shows."

Television! Yet another thing we don't have at

the North Pole. Reading about the invention and the various types of programming created for the device always sparked my curiosity. No need to tell him that. "I wasn't thinking clearly. I was so worried about Betty. And then I saw my pen." The horrible memory rushes back, and the stress of the evening overwhelms me. Tears leak from the corners of my eyes as my shoulders quiver.

Sven pats my back, possibly more firmly than he intends, and offers some words of comfort. "It doesn't count for much, but I believe you, eh? I'm sure the deputies will find some evidence to clear you. Let's hope."

A sobering thought slows my tears. "What if they don't? What if they don't find a piece of evidence to clear my name? What happens?"

Sven shakes his head. "Then I suppose there'll be a miscarriage of justice, miss. I can't see them putting you in prison for a crime you didn't commit, but—"

"Prison!" My heart flutters with fear.

He stops the truck in front of the bakery and pats my shoulder one more time. "The door should still be open. Medical examiner and probably a deputy or two are still gathering evidence from the crime scene. I recommend you mind your own business and go straight to your apartment. I'm sure Ronnie will be by in the morning to talk to you. He was a deputy for thirty-five years. He'll give you good advice. Even if it is a little outdated."

"Thank you for getting me out of there, Sven. I know you told me I have to charge for my cookies, but you and your family can have free cookies for life." Tears once again gather at the corners of my eyes.

"That's not necessary, you know. But much appreciated. Good night, miss."

As I open the door and trudge up the stairs, voices from Betty's apartment send a chill across my skin. Sven told me it was the medical examiner and deputies, but part of me worries the killer has returned.

Quietly opening my door, I slip into the apartment, close the door behind me, and drive the deadbolt home.

My foolish, trusting nature seems out of place tonight.

"Artikoa? Artikoa, are you here?"

There's a soft yelp from the corner of the room behind the dresser.

As I approach my traveling trunk, another yelp echoes from inside.

When I open the lid, Artikoa leaps free. "Thank you. I was lucky you left the trunk lid open. It makes a great hiding spot. Once I got inside, I was too short to get any leverage. Who knows how long I would've been trapped in there if you hadn't come back? By the way, why are you back?"

I share the gift of Ronnie's generosity and Sven's kindness.

"Glad to see there are some good humans left in the world. Whoever attacked Betty certainly isn't one of them."

"They charged me with murder."

"I assumed. They rarely set bail on the innocent. When is your arraignment?" Artikoa makes himself comfortable in the green-velvet chair.

The wrinkled, tear-soaked paper in my hand suddenly feels like a cold mug of cocoa. Smoothing it on the kitchen table, I count on my fingers.

"Looks like it will be next Tuesday. A week from today. What should I do?"

"I fear the best option is to locate the actual killer."

"You can't be serious! I don't want to find a killer! What if they come after me?"

"I'm not suggesting you advertise what you're up to, Cynthia. However, the most convincing method of proving your innocence will be to produce the guilty party."

Dropping my head into my hands, I moan. "You actually think I'll have better luck solving this crime than the sheriff's deputies?"

"You may lack experience, but you are highly motivated. Plus, you have proven to be an intelligent woman. That delivery route you planned for your father three years ago wasn't luck or an accident. You evaluated all the factors and came up with a wonderful plan. Solving this crime is the same idea. Collect all the information available and then draw the most convincing conclusion. You know you didn't hurt Betty, so that already puts you a step ahead of law enforcement."

"If you say so. I'd sure like to figure out how that pen I gave Mitch wound up in Betty's neck." I shiver and shake my hands to banish the image.

"The most likely conclusion would be that Mitch put it there. You've already got your first lead." He tilts his head.

"Thank you, Artikoa. I know you were against this venture into the human world from the start, and it would be very easy to abandon me. Thanks for not doing that."

Moping toward my bed, I tuck myself under the covers, but my eyes refuse to close.

Artikoa leaps down from his cozy chair and hops on the bed. He curls up at the foot of the bed, with his head turned away from me. "Don't get used to it. It's only for tonight."

"Much appreciated." Despite the exhausting events of the evening, my eyelids seem determined to stay open, but eventually, sleep overtakes me.

My dreams are filled with unpleasant images and repeated flashes of the sinister hooded figure.

At breakfast, Artikoa gobbles down three eggs, while I can barely finish one gingerbread cookie.

"I'm going to head down to the grocery store and talk to Mitch. Should I tell him I'm investigating Betty's . . . murder?"

"I wouldn't recommend that. Just have a conversation with him. See if you can figure out what happened to the pen."

"You got it."

Grabbing a scarf and mittens from the trunk that recently served as Artikoa's hiding place, I take my keys and lock the apartment.

Yellow crime-scene tape covers the door to Betty's apartment, and I have to duck under more tape on the inside when I leave through our shared front door.

I also lock that door. Can't be too careful anymore.

The brisk walk to the grocery store clears some of the cotton candy from my head. When I step into the Piggly Wiggly, all heads turn.

Wow. News in Silver Shoals seems to travel even faster than news at the North Pole.

Shifting my gaze to the floor, I walk toward the

double doors and push the service button. A pang of sadness pokes my heart as I think of Betty and me standing here together so recently.

Mitch pushes through the doors with a smile. When he lays eyes on me, his expression quickly shifts. "Oh, I'm quite busy. You'll have to come back another day."

"Mitch, I only need a minute. And I didn't hurt Betty. I promise you. They made a mistake. I was trying to help her."

His frown softens, but his eyes are still filled with disbelief. "Fine. I have a couple minutes. What you need?"

"I was wondering if I could get that pen back? It's kind of special. I probably shouldn't have handed it off so quickly. I can get you another pen."

He shuffles his weight from one foot to the other and avoids looking directly into my eyes. "Someone took it. Sorry. If I had it, I would give it back. But it's missing. I don't know what happened to it."

"Missing? When did it disappear?"

Mitch clears his throat and wrings his hands. "Well, seems like it was the day after you were here. It was in my pen caddy, and then it wasn't. I've asked the staff, and no one has seen it."

Great. This feels like a dead end. Then, I remember all the people who come in and out of my father's office during the day. "Did you have any appointments after we spoke?"

Mitch struggles to remember and gazes off into the distance. "Yeah, sure did. I met with a couple of vendors. The guy who delivers the pet products and a rep from the paper goods. But I think the pen was still there after they left." The expression on Mitch's face shifts. He's genuinely interested in remembering now.

"Okay. Anybody else that day?"

"No. That was it, you know."

"Sure. What about yesterday? Anybody come in then?"

"Hmmm. Let's see . . . I had a performance review with my meat department manager . . . Sven came in to pick up payment for the sign he made for the deli . . . And I had to handle an emergency when power went out in one of the walk-in freezers. That's all I remember." He crosses his arms and rocks on his heels.

"Do you remember seeing your pen after you came back from fixing the freezer?"

Mitch's whole body shifts, and he squares his shoulders. "No! It was gone. That's when I noticed it was missing. Somebody must've been in my office while I was working on the cooler. You're quite a little detective, Cindy." His smile is genuine.

"I sure hope so. I've gotta find out who hurt Betty. Not just to clear my name. I want the person who— Well, I suppose I want justice."

Mitch inhales sharply. "Sorry, Cindy. I thought the worst of you without knowing the whole story. Real sorry."

Shrugging my shoulders, I smile warmly. "It's okay. I appreciate you talking to me, Mitch. And if you remember anything else, or find out who was in your office, you give me a call. Okay?"

He nods. "I suppose you still got the same phone number over there at the bakery, eh?"

"I think so. I placed my first call to 911."

Unpleasant images once again surface, and I thank Mitch for his time and rush out before fresh tears can fall.

When I walk up the step at the bakery, the door is ajar.

I'm sure I locked it when I left.

Someone's inside.

CHAPTER 11

My heart is thudding in my chest like the feet of a thousand elves tap dancing. A North Pole favorite.

Artikoa can take care of himself — unless the killer has a gun . . .

Papa always told me I was quiet as a mouse. The only person he knew that could ever sneak up on Santa. Time to test the theory.

Ducking under the crime-scene tape, I ease the door shut behind me and tiptoe toward the staircase. Hugging against the railing and walking on the more sturdy side of each step, rather than the squeaky center, I make it to the landing without a sound.

There are no voices, so whoever is up there is alone.

Alone, like me.

For a moment, I consider running out and asking to use the phone across the street. But if the person who hurt Betty has returned, I want to make sure I get a good look at them this time.

I'll peek through her door and retreat to the safety of my apartment before they even notice me. The perfect plan.

Using the same technique on the second flight of stairs, I make it to the top and inch toward Betty's partially open door. Peering around the corner, between two rows of crime-scene tape, I can only see the back of whoever is in the apartment.

Based on the size of the shoe and broad shoulders, it's most likely a man. As I lean to get a closer look, the floorboard beneath my snow boots squeaks, and the man turns sharply.

"Who's there? This is a crime scene. No one's allowed in here."

"Well, you're in there. Who are you?"

The man gets to his feet, scans me and my Christmas attire, and smiles. "You must be the neighbor I read about in the report. Nice to meet you, Cindy Claus. I'm Keith Winters, the medical examiner."

He extends a hand toward me, and I eagerly

grip his hand and shake it vigorously, as I learned from Ronnie.

"Nice to meet you, Mr. Winters. What are you doing back here?"

"Please, call me Keith. There were some anomalies in the evidence. I came back to see if I could provide myself with a better explanation."

"What kind of anomalies?"

He smiles. "It's not appropriate for me to discuss an ongoing investigation, Miss Claus."

His gaze causes me to blush. "You can call me Cindy. I might be able to help. Betty was a friend. The accusations against me are false. Honestly. I would never hurt Betty."

He nods. "My gut tells me you're right. The evidence is all over the place. I can probably ask you a couple of questions without compromising the investigation."

"Sure. I'm happy to help." A soft growl from my apartment causes my mouth to go dry. I'll keep going, for now. Keith Winters is definitely on the Nice List. And he's been so kind.

"This is probably going to sound a little nuts, but do you know if Betty kept any exotic pets?"

"Exotic? What do you mean?"

"Um, let's see . . . exotic pets means not your normal cat or dog. Sometimes these pets require special permits, but I checked the city records and couldn't find anything like that." He tilts his head to the side and narrows his gaze.

"Can you tell me what kind of pet you're looking for?"

Keith inhales, then shakes his head. "I couldn't. I've identified a follicle of animal fur that I found here, and this could be a critical piece of information for finding the killer. I don't know — I can't. I can't tell you."

"Was it an arctic fox?"

His eyes widen, and the look of friendliness slips away as suspicion creeps in. "Why do you ask?"

"Because after Betty screamed, I ran in and my dog followed me."

"This dog of yours, is he actually a dog?"

Icicles! I absolutely cannot lie to this man. "He's a family pet. He was my father's, and he was given to me for protection."

Keith chews the inside of his cheek and nods. "Could I have a look at this *dog*?"

A sharp yip echoes inside my apartment. "Yes, but can you give me a minute?"

Twisting the key in the lock, I open the door and slip in.

Artikoa paces angrily. His voice is a growling whisper. "What have you done? Don't you understand it's illegal to have an arctic fox as a pet?

They'll take me away and send me to some zoo. This will be all your fault!"

"I'm sorry. I can't lie, especially not to Keith. He seems like a decent man. I feel like he'll be fair. He only wants a sample of your fur."

Growl.

Opening my door wide, I smile at Keith. "Come on in. Artikoa isn't happy about this arrangement, but you can take a sample of his fur if you want. I think."

Mr. Winters chuckles and steps into the apartment. He's not aggressive or insistent. He sits on the floor and offers Arti a friendly nod. "Hey, buddy. Been through a lot these last few days, eh? Witnessing a murder is never easy, whether you're human or animal. If I could grab a couple of hairs from your back, it would be a huge help. I need to eliminate the possibility that the killer was wearing some kind of fox-fur stole."

At the mention of fur clothing, Artikoa growls fiercely.

"Hey, I'm on your side, buddy. Personally, I would never ever wear fur. I only need a couple of hairs. We'll pull them out with these tweezers, put them in an evidence bag, and you'll probably never see me again."

Artikoa creeps toward Keith, and the entire scene warms my heart. The man is being so kind and gentle with Artikoa, yet there's something more. Something in my tummy. Cinnamon Roll used to call them good vibes. It's not only because Keith is on the Nice List. He's a lovely human being.

Eventually, Artikoa closes the distance and allows Keith to collect the evidence. There are two soft yelps as the tweezers yank the samples from his back, but no nips or growls.

"Thank you, Artikoa. Cool name, by the way." Keith stands and faces me. "This will really help us."

"Good. Great." I don't know what to do with my hands.

"Thanks for doing me this favor, Cindy. I'm glad I didn't have to get a warrant. I feel like I owe you."

"Nonsense. I'm happy to help with the investigation. I want to find whoever did this as much as you. I don't feel safe here, knowing that there's someone so dangerous loose in Silver Shoals."

He leans back on his heels and gazes at me with a combination of admiration and something I can't put my finger on. "Cindy, for what it's worth, I don't think you did this. Maybe I'm not a great judge of character, but you don't seem the type. I'm gonna let you in on an unfortunate piece of information. There were three sets of prints on the pen that were used as a murder weapon. Yours, the victim's, and Mitch Donaldson's."

"Oh, I gave the pen to Mitch. So that makes sense. I don't think Betty ever touched it, though . . . I can't quite remember."

"A deputy spoke to Mitch. He claims the pen was stolen from his office. With the obvious winter weather around here, seems like whoever took it was wearing gloves."

"Yeah, that makes sense. Mitch was trying to remember all the people who'd been in his office, but it was a pretty long list."

Keith smiles and glances over my shoulder. "Are those gingerbread cookies?"

"Yes. I'm testing out new recipes, and this is from Connie Schmenkel's cookbook. Ronnie gave me a couple of them when he found out I was opening a bakery."

He smiles and takes a step. "May I?"

"Of course." As I turn to grab the plate of cookies from the table, Keith elaborates.

"There were some gingerbread cookies found at the crime scene, but we're not allowed to eat those."

Chuckling as I return with the plate, I have to clarify. "Those I made from memory, from a recipe from . . . an old family recipe. Connie's are better."

He takes a cookie with thick icing, bites into it,

and smiles as he chews. "Oh boy! These are better than my grandma used to make. Wow! You can be sure I'll be back to your bakery on a regular basis." He finishes the cookie and scrunches up his face as he reaches toward the plate.

"Take as many as you like. I can always make more." He takes two more cookies and enjoys every mouthful. "I need to get back to the lab and make sure these fibers match what we found at the crime scene. If they do, you may need to get a permit for your *dog*."

"I don't know how to do that."

He sniffs, taps his fingers on his leg, and sighs. "I'll think of something. No need to stir up more trouble for you. I know you're already trying to beat a murder rap."

Our eyes meet, and the mirth quickly drains from mine. "Yeah. And I've got to do it before next Tuesday."

"Well, if you bribe me with cookies, I'm happy to keep you up to date on any breaks we have in the case. As long as you do the same for me."

I use a phrase I've heard several times since my arrival. "You betcha."

Keith lifts a cookie in thanks and departs.

"He seemed nice, don't you think, Artikoa?"

"I will reserve judgment. I'm not especially fond of people who yank my fur out by the roots."

"Sorry about that. I couldn't think of any other way to help the investigation."

"You may have helped the investigation, but you unleashed a world of trouble for us. If he reports your possession of an exotic animal, we may have to get your father involved."

"Blizzards! I don't want Papa's help. I can handle this. Keith is on the Nice List. I know he'll find a way. At least, I hope he finds a way."

"Yes. You and I both." Artikoa hops onto the cozy green chair, sits proudly, and curls his fluffy white tail around his feet.

"Did you hear what he said about the pen?"

"Are you referring to the human fingerprints?"

"Yeah. Mine, Mitch's, and Betty's? I'm certain she didn't touch the pen. I was using it, and then I handed it directly to Mitch. There's no way her prints would be on that pen, unless . . ."

"Unless Betty went back to Mitch's office later and took the pen."

"Artikoa! She's not a thief."

"Maybe she isn't, but you should look into it. I didn't make the connection before, but her apartment was filled with too many different scents. Either she does a heap of entertaining, or there are a number of things in that apartment which don't belong to her."

"Now you're accusing her of multiple thefts? First, it was just the pen. Oh dear!"

Artikoa circles once and curls against the velvet.

"I better go talk to Sherman Canton. I know he's her ex-boyfriend now, but he might be able to give me some insight into who Betty was and who she hung out with. At least then I'll know who to talk to."

As I head to the door, he yips once.

"What is it? Are you hungry?"

"Not presently, but I needed your attention. Due to recent events, and the possible threat of animal control, or worse, I'd like to have an escape route."

"Escape? From where?"

"I believe they're called dog doors." He shakes violently at the word. "But we should get one installed in the apartment door and another beside the front door. I'm sure they craft doors that can be secured, so when we're safely inside we can lock it, but should the need arise for me to make myself scarce, I'd like to know it was possible."

"No problem. I'll stop in at the hardware store after I finish talking to Sherman. Do you want to join me?"

"Actually, I would. I could use some fresh air. If you don't mind, I like to head off on my own and explore the surrounding wilderness. I may take care of finding my own supper today."

"Yuck. I don't mean to judge, but please don't tell me about it." I have to swallow the acid in my throat.

"It's how things work in nature, Cynthia. The system has functioned for millennia."

"Fine. Follow me."

We head down the stairs and get a nice surprise — for a change.

Ronnie waits on the sidewalk. "Hey there. I was just about to knock."

"Ronnie! Thank you so much for bailing me out. Sven said you'd be by."

"Yup. Yup. He mentioned you're going to look into things. I worked in that station for thirty-five years, and I can tell you corners get cut. You let me know if you need any help with any of the deputies."

"I will. As a matter of fact, I just met Keith Winters. He seems nice."

"Retired before he came on board. But I've heard good things."

"Oh! Wait here." Running back inside, I grab a bag of gingerbread cookies and bring them out for Ronnie. "Here's the first recipe I tried. I hope you like them."

He sighs deeply and nods. "The icing looks nice and thick. Connie would be proud."

"I haven't gotten to the rye bread yet, but I will."

Ronnie smiles. "Wishing you all the best on the investigation, Cindy." He turns and hobbles down the hill.

"Thanks again for the bail."

He doesn't turn, but lifts one hand and waves it away as though it were nothing.

I lock the bakery and hurry across the street to Sherman's café.

The young hostess recognizes me and offers a dutiful smile. "No pets allowed."

Artikoa steps outside and waits at the bottom of the step. His expression is one of tolerance.

"Oh, we're not staying. I was hoping to talk to Sherman."

She arches one eyebrow. "Sherman is prepping for the dinner service. He doesn't like to be interrupted."

"I understand. It's about Betty."

The girl's blue eyes widen, and she shuffles off toward the kitchen.

Less than a minute later, a tall man with a generous belly and blond hair gathered into a low pony, pushes through the swinging door and stops to size me up.

"I have a couple minutes. Follow me upstairs."

I follow him up two flights of stairs to a large landing.

"This is about Betty? What kind of trouble has she stirred up now?"

"None. She's dead."

He rears back as though he's been slapped and tugs on his ponytail. "When? I just talked to her yesterday about the prep kitchen expansion. Are you sure?"

Images I don't care to see flash through my mind. "Oh, I'm very sure. In fact, the medical examiner just left." Pointing out the window, I gesture to the tape. "See the crime scene tape?"

Sherman fusses with a button on his chef's coat. "Shame. I always told her that her nosy nature would get her into trouble."

"What do you mean?"

He shrugs and exhales. "I don't mean to speak ill of the dead, but Betty could be a troublemaker. She loved to gossip, and occasionally, she uncovered a real nugget. Between that and her kleptomania, she got on the wrong side of a few folks."

My brain is scanning through years of vocabulary words. "Betty liked to steal things? Did she not have enough money?"

"That had nothing to do with it. Her yarn shop did okay. And she had a decent settlement from a medical malpractice lawsuit she won about a decade ago. She didn't take things because she needed them. The way she explained it to me was that there was some kind of thrill in slipping things into her pocket and no one noticing."

"How strange." Shrugging, I continue. "I've never met anyone like that before. She didn't take anything from me."

"I wouldn't be too sure. If you've got the key to her apartment, you should probably have a look around."

"I don't. And I wouldn't. It's a crime scene. Deputies said no one is allowed in."

Sherman scoffs. "The deputies. You mean the Keystone Cops? Saul Rivera hasn't run a clean investigation since the day he was put in charge. I feel sorry for whoever gets accused of this crime. Doesn't take much evidence to convict anyone in this town."

A yip from the sharp-eared Artikoa outside reaches me, but I hardly need the reminder. There's no way I'm going to mention I'm the prime suspect. "Betty said that you two were still friends even though you'd broken up. In fact, she said you even let her use your truck sometimes."

Sherman's face reddens, and his hands ball into fists. "That's what happened to my spare keys! I should've known. To be clear, I broke up with her.

And I never said anything about her using my truck."

There's an angry energy coming off him, and I can tell he's awful upset about Betty taking his keys. "I'm sure if you let the deputies know your keys are missing, they can check the apartment for you."

He blows air through his lips and rolls his eyes. "Not likely. As you may have gathered, I'm not a fan of Saul Rivera. And he's no fan of mine." Sherman wraps his arms across his chest, as a talisman against the drafty building, and rubs some warmth into his body. "I gotta get back to the kitchen. Was there anything else?"

"I didn't know Betty that well. It seems like she was in the habit of upsetting people. Do you know anyone who would've been angry enough to do something like this?"

He sighs heavily. "She had something on the mayor. I know that. And the owner of the laundromat was no fan of hers. Have you tried talking to the gals at the bingo club? That group drinks a lot during bingo. And there's nothing like alcohol to pry the truth from someone's lips."

"I'll talk to them. Thanks for your time. And I'm sorry for your loss."

Sherman wrinkles up his face and tilts his head. "You're new in town, right?"

"That's right. I'm opening a bakery and just getting settled."

He glances across the street. "Oh, you're *that* Cindy. You ruined my perfectly good plans for expansion. Well, I'd wish you luck, but part of me hopes you fail. Nothing personal. I just need a larger space for my restaurant."

With that, he turns and jogs down the steps to the café.

"Thanks, I think."

As soon as the door closes behind me, Artikoa growls. "I do not care for Sherman."

"Yeah, he's definitely on the Naughty List. Although, he did provide some useful information about possible enemies of Betty."

"I'd like to head to the woods. It's getting dark. Perhaps you best follow the rest of your leads tomorrow."

"Maybe. I'm going to check the newspaper, though. I thought I saw something about bingo on Saturday nights. Might be time for me to learn a human pastime."

Artikoa offers a high-pitched whine, which sounds like a potential objection. Shrugging my shoulders, I return to the bakery as he races off for his woodland adventure.

CHAPTER 12

*W*HAT DOES ONE WEAR to a bingo parlor? Papa loves the game of bingo, and the elves hold weekly bingo games with prizes ranging from sweet treats to extra shifts at the toy factory. It might sound like a strange reward to a human, but elves really love making toys.

Anyway, a green pair of my warm winter leggings and a fun Christmas sweater dress should do the trick.

Remembering the chill I experienced before Sven loaned me his coat, I grab an extra thick sweater to wear over my fancy one. Add a hat and gloves, and I'm all set.

I'll have to locate a store in town that sells clothing and get myself a warm winter coat. I miss the North Pole and being surrounded by my mother's magic, but experiencing changes in temperature for the first time is quite exciting.

The newspaper gave an address for the bingo hall. Fortunately, as Santa's daughter, I have a flawlessly accurate sense of direction. It takes nearly fifteen minutes to walk to a place called the Elk's Lodge. As I draw near, warm light spills from the windows and raucous laughter floats out each time the doors open.

Stepping inside, two women at a table greet me. "Well, how do you do? How many cards do you want?"

"Would you believe this is my first time playing bingo?" I leave out the part about in the human world. "Can you give me any pointers?"

The women debate the finer points of two cards versus four and finally seem to agree.

"Since you're a beginner, it makes the most sense to start with two cards. That'll be enough to keep you busy for tonight. You listen for the calls, and then you use this little stamper to mark your card."

Gazing at the cards, I think I have the hang of it. "So if they call B-6, I should stamp both cards?"

"You sure do," the woman with strawberry-blonde hair says.

"You're practically a pro," the lady with grey curls chimes in.

The women exchange a friendly chuckle.

Handing them some of my paper money, they give me change and two cards.

I dug one of my childhood purses from the bottom of my traveling trunk. The strap looks like reindeer horns, and the big red-button fastener is a dead ringer for Rudolph's nose. Now that I have to carry things with me when I leave the house, like keys and cash, I need something to keep them in.

"Isn't that the cutest purse you've ever seen?" The ladies smile and point.

"Thank you. It was a gift from my father."

"You don't say? Your father must be the best gift giver this side of the Mississippi!"

I'll have to check a map to refresh my memory on the details of the Mississippi, but she's right about my papa. He's the best gift-giver in the entire world. "He really is. Wish me luck."

Both of the ladies give me a thumbs up, and I wander into the hall, searching for any sign of the women Sherman referred to as "the gals."

Several of the tables have filled up, but there are five women standing at the bar raising a toast.

As I walk closer, I hear Betty's name. This could be my lucky night.

"Excuse me. Did I hear you mention Betty? She was my across-the-hall neighbor."

The women lower their glasses, and their easy grins are quickly replaced with a variety of frowns.

Nice. Naughty. Naughty. Nice. Naughty. Betty certainly kept interesting company.

The tall brunette is the first to respond. "Oh, sorry, we didn't mean it. Betty was a sweetheart."

I hadn't heard what they said before Betty's name, but based on the defensive reaction, it must not have been good. "Oh, I only knew her for a few days. I'm new in town." I was coming to understand: I only knew the good side of Betty. "Was she close to all of you?"

Guilty looks and mumbles race through the circle.

The brunette in a dark-green hoodie steps forward. "Hi, I'm Tawny. Betty was a regular at the bingo hall, and she could be a lot of fun. Unfortunately, once she had a few—" She looks helplessly at the other girls, so I jump in.

"She has a tendency to gossip?"

They breathe a collective sigh of relief. A grey-blonde woman with big curls is the next to speak. "Hi, I'm Claudette. Didn't catch your name."

"It's Cindy. Nice to meet you."

Claudette continues. "Can I be perfectly honest with you, Cindy?"

"Of course." I lean toward her, hoping for a useful tidbit.

"We were all wondering when the deputies would be done at her apartment. A couple of us would like to get in there and see if we can find some things that have gone missing over the years."

This is the second mention of Betty's tendency to take things that didn't belong to her. I'm beginning to wonder if she stole the gold pen from Mitch, and the killer simply grabbed a weapon of opportunity once they were in her apartment.

"The crime scene tape is still up. I have to duck under it at the front door every day when I go home. And I won't be able to open my bakery until they're finished."

Claudette gasps and clutches her chest. "Bakery! Oh, my goodness. Croissants and coffee. Please tell me you'll be serving coffee?"

"I wish I could. I hadn't thought of it. I don't really have room right now. I'll probably just start with my baked goods and see where that leads."

Tawny grips my shoulder. "Gosh, I'm sure you could expand into the yarn shop now that Betty's gone."

I don't care for the snickers that ripple through the crowd.

"I'm happy where I'm at. I better find a place to sit. Nice to meet all of you."

The women nod, but as I step away, Claudette calls out. "Let us know when they're done with the investigation, won't you? Someone will have to pack up all of her things."

The thought had never occurred to me; that the apartment would have to be emptied. "Doesn't Betty have any family?"

Tawny fields this question. "The way we heard it, she was an only child. Her parents were kinda old when they had her, and they've both passed away. If the cops need someone to clear the place out, you let them know we all volunteered."

Their misguided motives aside, I don't want to get involved. "If they ask, I'll let them know."

Looking through the rows of tables, I eventually find an empty chair.

Placing my two cards in front of me, I settle in as the caller climbs onto the stage and walks toward the microphone. "Alright, ladies and gents. Let's get started." He grabs the handle on the cage filled with balls and cranks it several times.

Then he opens the door, reaches in, and extracts one ball. "Our first call is B-6."

Wait. That was the number I used in my example when I was talking to— Oh well. Taking my little stamper, I daub the B-6 square on both of my cards.

Wonder if he'll call N-33 next? Not sure why that popped into my head.

"The next call is N-33."

Whoa. I'm not sure if I'm influencing the call or having some kind of premonition. Either way, I don't think it's good. Maybe G-45? Stop, Cindy. Stop.

"Are you ladies ready for the next call?" The crowd claps uproariously. "That'll be G-45!"

How about my I-17? My heart is racing, and beads of sweat break out along my hairline. I should probably stop, but curiosity is killing me.

"The next one is I-17."

Well, if the next call is O-61, I'll have a bingo.

"Remember, ladies, the first bingo of the night is a double bonus win. Here's our next call. O-61."

Getting to my feet, I lift my card and wave it like the ladies told me. "Bingo. I have a bingo."

Several people clap, but the majority seem to groan or grumble.

This whole thing is very confusing. Bingo at the North Pole is more supportive. Everyone wants to win, but no one's upset if they lose.

"Bring your card up to the checker. Once we verify that bingo, you can buy yourself a new card or cash out."

Taking my card up to the woman sitting beside the stage, she verifies my bingo and signs her name on the card.

She points at the bar. "You take this over to the bar, sweetie. You got $100 coming your way."

I'm still not entirely sure whether that's a lot of money or a little. I offer a friendly smile and take my card to the bar.

The bartender congratulates me, hands me my cash, and takes my card. He tears the card in half and throws it in the trash. "Can't have someone trying to redeem the same card twice, now, can we?"

"Of course not. That would be dishonest."

He chuckles and nods.

Maybe I should leave. I uncovered a little information from the bingo gals, won some money, and should probably leave before I give myself another bingo.

Returning to my chair for a moment, I grab my purse and whisper goodbye to the ladies seated on either side of me. They wave distractedly, but don't remove their eyes from their bingo cards.

As I walk home, I worry that I may have made more enemies than friends. Knowing the numbers ahead of time was certainly strange. Maybe Artikoa will have more information on that.

As I trudge up the steep sidewalk toward the

bakery, a light from the window catches my eye. It's not the window above the bakery. It's Betty's place.

Maybe Keith Winters came back to get something.

Thinking happy thoughts as I approach the door, all my positivity vanishes when I see the shattered glass that used to be our front door.

Keith never would've broken the glass. The killer might be back.

Racing across the street to Sherman's café, I pound on the door even though the sign says closed.

An angry Sherman stomps from the back room and doubles down on his frown when he catches sight of me.

Finally opening the door, I push myself inside. "I need to use your phone. There's an intruder in Betty's apartment."

His irritation rapidly shifts to concern. "Who is it?"

"I have no idea. I was coming back from bingo. I saw the light. The glass in the front door was broken. It's not one of the deputies or the medical examiner." My breath is coming in quick gasps.

"Take some deep breaths. Calm down." Sherman takes the lead. "Follow me. Phone's right there."

Pressing the numbers Artikoa taught me, I explain the situation as soon as the woman on the other end answers.

"That's right. Betty Troup's apartment. Above the yarn shop on Main Street. Where there was that recent . . . incident."

She verifies the information and tells me to stay on the line until the deputies arrive. She asks if I can see my front door from where I'm standing. "No, I can't. Hold on. Sherman, can you go watch the door? If the person leaves, they want to know if they get into a car."

"Of course. You stay on the phone."

There must not be much happening in Silver Shoals this time of night. Deputies arrive in less than two minutes. Sherman turns to notify me. "Two deputies just ran into the building."

Ending my call to the dispatcher, I join Sherman by the window.

Sooner than I would've imagined, the two deputies return, pushing a man in handcuffs in front of them.

"Do you recognize that guy, Sherman?"

Sherman whistles and shakes his head. "That's the mayor. The mayor of Silver Shoals caught in a B&E. I bet that'll be front page news tomorrow."

"What was the mayor doing in Betty's apartment?"

Sherman's gaze hardens, and his eyes take on a steely glint. "I told you she wasn't as nice as she pretended to be. She didn't just take things. Sometimes she'd find things out about people and use it against them. For money."

"Blackmail? Betty was blackmailing people?"

Sherman scoffs. "Yeah. Good little Betty Boop. Not all she was cracked up to be."

"I thought her last name was Troup?"

"Inside joke." He shrugs. "You got someplace to stay?"

"Things should be okay now. I need to go check on my dog. Oh, who do I call about fixing the glass?"

"Frida at the hardware store can hook you up. She knows a couple of handy guys that do odd jobs for her." He opens the door. "You sure you'll be okay tonight?"

"Well, if the mayor was the killer, then I should be safe."

Sherman looks surprised. "Yeah, I hadn't thought about that. Maybe that story in the paper tomorrow will mention more than the B&E."

"Thank you for letting me use your phone. Good night, Sherman."

"Yeah, good night."

He locks the door behind me, and I hurry

across the street and up the stairs to my apartment.

My door is secure. However, the door to Betty's apartment is smashed off the frame.

"Artikoa, are you okay? I'm alone."

The fox's reassuring voice sounds through the door. "I'm fine. Did they catch the man who broke into Betty's apartment?"

"They did." Unlocking the apartment door, I let him come out to survey the damage. "It was the mayor. Sherman says that Betty might've been blackmailing him! And when I talked to the ladies at bingo tonight, they mentioned her stealing things from them. I don't think Betty was as nice a person as she pretended to be. What's a B&E?"

Artikoa sniffs the air for a moment and glances up at me. "It's short for breaking and entering. Which is what the mayor definitely did. However, since he did the hard work for us, perhaps we should take advantage of this opportunity to search the apartment."

"Wait! What are you suggesting?"

"I'm suggesting that you're running out of time to prove your innocence, and this might be our only opportunity to find a critical clue. Now, leave your gloves on, close her curtains, and use your mother's magic to create a ball of light. I know you can do it. I saw you use it as a child when you wanted to stay up past your bedtime reading."

I haven't thought about those days in so long. Actually, I'm not sure I can even remember how to do it. Tiptoeing across the threshold, I close the heavy curtains on Betty's front windows. Then, rolling one hand over the other, I summon a ball of light in the darkness. It takes several tries, but eventually, the long-buried memory surfaces, and I'm able to create the sphere of illumination to help us search.

Artikoa follows his nose and is the first to uncover a critical clue.

"What is it?"

He tips his nose at a book. "Something in this carries the scent of the man who broke in."

Reaching for the book with one hand, I tip it upside down and fan the pages. A folded paper flutters to the floor. Reaching for the paper, I unfold it and show it to Artikoa. "What is it?"

"That's a check. And it's a check for $10,000 from the mayor to Betty. Looks like Sherman was right about her blackmail scheme."

"What about the things she took from other people? Maybe someone else had more of a reason to harm her than the mayor."

Together, we continue to locate items that don't smell of Betty. By the end of our search, we have uncovered jewelry from at least five different people, a wallet, and a driver's license with a picture of Sherman, but bearing someone else's name entirely.

"What should we do with all this stuff?"

"It should be turned over to the deputies, but if you report it, they'll know you were sniffing around the apartment."

"Actually, you were the one sniffing, Arti. I was only grabbing stuff you found. Plus, I had my gloves on the whole time, so I didn't put fingerprints on anything. Maybe we could lay everything out on the table, and I can mention the intruder to Keith."

Artikoa pauses, looks at me, and cocks his head sideways. "Oh, it's Keith, is it?"

"What?"

"I didn't realize you and the medical examiner were on a first-name basis."

"Don't tease me. I promised to let him know if I found any other clues. We're sort of doing each other a favor, understand?"

The sly fox seems to snicker. "I understand perfectly."

Artikoa and I collect everything we can, lay the items one by one on a small table, and, once we've safely returned to my apartment, I place a call to Keith.

CHAPTER 13

*A*FTER LETTING KEITH KNOW about the B&E, Artikoa and I enjoy a late-night snack while we wait for Mr. Winters to arrive.

Footsteps on the stairs outside give me a case of chills, even though I feel certain they belong to Keith.

Knock, knock, knock.

"Who is it?"

"Hey, Cindy. It's me, Keith."

"Just a minute." For some reason, I feel compelled to check my hair in the mirror. Artikoa growls. "You look fine. Answer the door."

I unlock the door and open it with a flourish. "Hi, Keith. Thanks for coming."

"You look nice. Do you have somewhere to be at this late hour, or are you just getting back?"

Giggling nervously, I brush at my fancy sweater dress. "Thanks. I went to the bingo— not important. You can see what a mess it is across the hall."

"Geez. Somebody really wanted to get in there. You said the deputies took someone out in handcuffs. You were right about it being the mayor. Can't imagine what he was doing in Betty's apartment, though."

Pinching my lips together, I shrug.

"Why don't you go back inside and lock your door? I'll let you know what I find in there."

"We—"

Artikoa yips loudly.

"Yup. Okay. I'll be in my apartment." Stepping inside, I close the door and press my cool hands to my flushed cheeks.

"Cynthia, were you about to disclose that we'd already been in the apartment?"

"I was. I don't know what it is about him? Thanks for saving me."

Artikoa hops into the cozy green chair and sits proudly. "It's becoming quite a habit."

Waiting for Keith to knock on the door sends me straight to baking. Whipping up a batch of lemon-drop cookies is the perfect distraction.

Before long, I'm humming away and the oven is preheating nicely.

Knock, knock, knock.

"Just a minute."

Stopping the mixer, I wipe my hands on the kitchen towel and carry it with me to the door.

"Are you baking? At this time of night?" Keith's green eyes dance with mirth.

"Baking calms me down. It's my happy place."

He chuckles as he drags his hand through his short black hair. "Do you need anybody to sample anything?"

"You're welcome to come in for a minute. I just have to throw this batch in the oven, and in about fifteen minutes you'll be eating warm cookies."

He pats his stomach. "Sounds good to me. A little extra weight through the winter never hurt anyone. Gotta stay warm any way you can."

Next thing you know, I'm giggling like an elf half my age. "Okay. That's the first tray in the oven."

Removing my apron, I join Keith in the seating area. However, with one of my two chairs occupied by Artikoa and one occupied by Keith, I'm left with no option other than sitting on the bed. Which makes me oddly self-conscious. Not something I've experienced before in my life.

"Those are really smelling good, Cindy. You're dangerous."

"Me? No. I'm as gentle as a newborn reindeer. I wouldn't hurt anyone. And I definitely didn't hurt Betty."

Keith leans forward and waves his hands. "I didn't mean it that way, Cindy. I meant your delicious baking is going to add more pounds to my middle than I'm prepared to handle."

"Oh . . . that kind of dangerous. My papa always says without my cookies— Never mind. What did you find next door?"

Keith licks his lip as he leans back in the chair. "It was quite an interesting find, actually. There were seven pieces of women's jewelry, a wallet, a check, and a driver's license, all carefully lined up on the table. The thing that I can't figure out is at least a couple of those pieces of jewelry were reported stolen, and the check for $10,000 was made out to Betty from the mayor."

I can't make eye contact. He'll see right through me. So I look up at the ceiling and twiddle my thumbs. "Wow. Sounds like that could be some useful evidence."

"Sure. You betcha. I'm sure the deputies will be pleased. The thing that's got me stumped is if the mayor broke into the apartment, it was probably to get that check back. Why he'd leave it lying on the table, I can't imagine. Any thoughts?"

I struggle to swallow. "That is strange."

Artikoa growls softly.

"Easy, boy. We're on the same side. I'm not all that interested in how the evidence came to be so well organized. I'm more interested in getting it into the deputies' hands."

Ping.

"That's the timer. Hold on to your Christmas stockings."

Keith chuckles as I run into the kitchen and pull the tray of cookies from the oven. Rather than letting them cool on the tray or rack, I slide them onto the counter and carefully place two piping-hot cookies on a plate.

"They're supposed to have icing. But I'm pretty sure you'll like them this way, too."

"I'm sure I will." Keith picks up a cookie, takes a large bite, and smiles as he inhales. "They taste even better than they smell. You're a wizard in the kitchen, Cindy. If there's going to be any reserved seating at that bakery of yours, please book me a table every day."

My cheeks blush with heat, and I glance at the floor. "Thank you. Thank you so much for saying that. It's been a crazy week. I hope some of this evidence will clear my name. I would really rather work in my bakery than sit in prison."

Keith's expression sobers as he finishes his last cookie. "I'll do everything I can to help clear your name, Cindy. Which reminds me, I better run down to my car and grab some evidence bags." He takes the plate to the kitchen, washes it, and places it in the drain bin. "It would be helpful if I knew where the various items had been found in the apartment. Any ideas?"

Artikoa growls, but part of me can't help but trust this wonderful man who's definitely on the top of my Nice List.

"If you are asking my opinion. Seems like the jewelry would've been in her jewelry box. Just a thought. And the wallet may have been tucked in an old blue purse in her closet. And as far as the check, that was probably stuck between a couple pages in one of the books on her coffee table."

"And the driver's license with the picture of Sherman, but a different name?"

"Seems like that would've been in the wallet. Right?"

Keith smiles and offers me a wink nearly as warm as one of my papa's. "Those sound like great ideas to me. Thanks for calling."

"No problem. I promised to let you know if I came across anything."

He chuckles as he leaves the apartment. "It's good to know you keep your word, Cindy Claus. Now, be sure to lock this door behind me."

"You got it."

Arti and I listen to Keith head down the stairs to get evidence bags, return, and once again exit.

After icing all the lemon-drop cookies, cleaning the kitchen, and packing the cookies away, it's time to sleep.

I crawl into bed, exhausted. Plus, I'm happy to report that for the second night in a row, Artikoa joins me on the antique brass bed.

SUNDAY MORNING IS OVERCAST, and a weight seems to press down on my shoulders. A cheery sweater with a jolly likeness of my father might lift my spirits.

Despite a healthy breakfast of lemon-drop cookies for me and coddled eggs for Artikoa, there's still an emptiness inside me when I bundle up and head out to the hardware store.

A short woman with black curly hair and a ready smile greets me as soon as I walk in.

"Hi. Sherman said you might know someone who could fix the broken glass in the front door at my bakery?"

"New in town? I'm Frida."

"Cindy. Nice to meet you."

Fortunately, Frida lifts my spirits with the great news that she knows someone who could repair my broken glass, and they work on Sundays.

"That's wonderful. Do you have their phone number?"

"Even better." She turns and shouts. "Justin?"

A man with shaggy blond hair walks out from the room behind the counter. "Yeah, boss?"

"This young lady has had some vandalism at her property. Can you grab your gear and head up there to fix some broken door glass?"

"You betcha. Where am I headed, boss?"

Frida smiles as she gestures to me. "This is Cindy. She's opening the bakery next to that yarn shop."

The young man rubs his scraggly mustache and frowns. "Didn't someone get murdered in there?"

"That was next door. I'm hoping the new evidence the deputies got last night will help bring the killer to justice." Hopefully, those vague details will be enough to convince him . . .

"Sounds good. Be up there in about ten minutes. Does that work for you?"

"Can you make it twenty? I have to stop at the laundromat on my way home."

Frida leans on the counter. "Mind your P's and Q's over there. That Todd can be a bit cranky if he hasn't had his medicine. If you know what I mean."

Based on Betty's gossip about the man having trouble with drink, I assume Frida is referring to the same thing.

"Thanks. I'll mind my letters."

When I step outside, and Artikoa and I get far enough away from the building to safely have a conversation, I ask about P's and Q's, and learn yet another human saying.

"There should be a book of these, Artikoa. Seems like I'm learning two or three new ones every day! How will I ever keep track?"

"It will become second nature soon enough. You're a natural at learning languages. This is just another version of English. They call it slang."

"Slang. Slang." A fit of giggles grips me. "Slang. It's kind of a fun word to say. How do you know so much about humans?"

"You forget, I've been around for centuries. Becoming an expert on the dangers your father might face each Christmas Eve was my sworn duty. Unfortunately, I had to investigate much more of the naughty side of humanity than the nice. It's important for Santa to focus on the positive. In order to keep him safe, someone has to investigate the negative. That was my realm."

"Do you miss it?"

Artikoa softly comes to a stop beside me. "I don't think I do. I thought I would. It was the primary reason I was so against accompanying you to this place, but you're doing good work here. I've seen the way you cheer people up with your baked goods, and if we solve the mystery of Betty's death, we can bring some closure to the community in that regard as well."

"Hey, is that what humans call a win-win?"

Arti bobs his angular head, but rather than a verbal reply, he yips and points his nose at the approaching human.

The man is sweeping snow from the sidewalk in front of the laundromat. "Hi, are you Todd?"

"Who wants to know?"

"Oh, me."

"Yeah, I figured. Who are you?" His tone is angry, and I worry he may not have had his *medicine*.

"I'm Cindy. I run the new bakery in town. I was wondering if I could ask you a couple of questions about Betty?"

"Never heard of her." He continues sweeping and avoids my gaze.

"Oh, she did her laundry here all the time. Betty Troup. She owned the yarn shop."

"Oh, her. Why are you talking about her in the past tense?"

"Well, she died. I thought you'd heard."

He stops and leans on his broom as a strange grin lifts his cheeks. "Couldn't have happened to a nicer gal. I don't have much to say about her other than things always went missing from other people's dryers when she was around. I'm not saying she was a thief, but it sure was a suspicious coincidence."

"That's unfortunate. But it hardly seems something you'd wish someone dead for! Did you have something against Betty personally?"

"You're awful nosy."

"Sorry. You just seem to really dislike her. I wondered why?"

"Well, I don't mind telling you. Betty came in to do her laundry a few weeks ago, and I was having a sip in the back. She called the cops and said I was drunk in public. They arrested me for drunk and disorderly. Had my picture in the paper and everything. Some folks came in and told me they were so upset they were willing to drive all the way to Timber Town to do their laundry, rather than support a drunk." He spits on the sidewalk and twists the broom against the spittle.

"I'm sorry that happened, Todd. Did you go to Betty's apartment to confront her?"

"What? I don't even know where she lives, kid. You and your dog better get outta here before I report you for leash-law violations." He picks up his broom and shakes it at me threateningly.

Artikoa growls, but I want to avoid any further confrontation.

"Thank you for your time, Todd. Would you like me to drop off some lemon-drop cookies later today?"

His features soften. "Did you say lemon drop?"

"That's right. Freshly made."

His entire expression changes, and, for a moment, I can almost see a younger, happier man.

"Those are my favorite cookies. My wife used to make those for me every Christmas — before the divorce."

"Well, I'm happy to bring you some Christmas Lemon Drops, Todd. Thanks again."

Artikoa and I climb the hill toward the bakeshop, and I sigh with relief. "That was a close one."

"It could've been. It seems you have a touch of your mother's gift of diplomacy, as well as your father's kindness. You are well suited for the human world, Cynthia."

"Thanks, Artikoa. That means a lot."

CHAPTER 14

*A*rtikoa is curled in a patch of sunlight just inside the bakery's front window, and I'm making another batch of lemon-drop cookies.

"Hey. It's Cindy, right?" Wiping my hands on my apron, I walk out of the kitchen. "Hi, Justin. I'm sure you can see where the glass needs to be replaced." We share a chuckle. "I wanted to ask you one more thing. Would it be possible to put a doggy door next to the front door, in that side-panel window, and another one in my apartment? Is that something you can handle?"

He steps out of the bakery and surveys the entrance to the foyer between my store and the yarn shop. "Should be possible. If we put it on the hinge side and equip it with a locking panel, that would keep you safe. Do you mind if I measure your dog? The doors come in various sizes."

"Artikoa, is it all right if the nice man measures you for a doggy door?"

Artikoa growls, and I feel bad that he must suffer the indignation of pretending to be what he considers a lower life form on the canine family tree.

"You'll be all right. He's grumpy, but he won't bite."

Justin slowly approaches, crouches, and holds his hand forward. "Give it a good sniff, pal. You'll see I'm friend, not foe."

Artikoa's gaze darts toward me, but he dutifully sniffs the hand and stands for the man.

The handyman takes a couple of quick measurements and smiles. "Good news. He's not much bigger than a Maine Coon, which is a pretty good-sized cat. I can get you a door that will fit perfectly in that panel beside the hinge side of the front door. And on the one for your apartment door, I'll build a barrier above it so no one can reach through and get to the lock on your door. I'll also adjust the locking panel on that one, so you can slide it in from the side. Okay. We're all set. Did you want all that handled today?"

I press a hand to my chest in shock. "I was thinking you might not even be able to finish the glass in the front door today. If you can do all of those things, I'd be thrilled. And I've got lemon-drop or gingerbread cookies to keep you going. Your choice."

Justin smiles and pats his flat stomach. "Thanks, but I've sworn off sugar. I know it's a strange time of year to do it, but my mom was diagnosed with diabetes last month, and I don't want to head down that road. I'd take a cup of coffee if you've got it."

"No problem. I'll be right back." As I jog up the steps to the apartment, a thought pops into my head. He's at least the third person who's mentioned coffee in the same breath as my bakery. Maybe my obsession with hot chocolate isn't going to be enough. I wonder what will happen to Betty's yarn shop. Icicles! I'm still accused of murder. This is not the time to be thinking about expansion.

It only takes a moment to brew a fresh pot of coffee, and when I return to the bottom of the steps, Justin has his sawhorses and tools spread all over the foyer.

"Here's your coffee."

"Thanks, Cindy. I apologize for letting in all the cold air. But I'll have that new glass up in a flash. Then I'll run back to the hardware store and grab those doggy doors."

Handing him a cup, I can't help but wonder

how old he is? Most humans would say he's my age, which they seem to think is around twenty-five. I have to ask. "Justin, how old are you?"

He chokes on his coffee and chuckles. "Funny! I know people ask women that all the time, but I can't think of the last time someone asked me. I'll be twenty-two at the end of the month. My birthday falls on New Year's Eve. It's a tough time of year to have a birthday — for a kid."

Never thought of it that way. Having my birthday on Christmas day always seemed magical. Before I can ask any follow-up questions, Keith Winters walks up the steps and through the opening where my front door used to be.

"Hey, Justin. I'm glad you're helping Cindy out. I'll feel a lot better once her door is repaired." He steps around the mini-construction site and gestures for me to follow him into the bakery.

"You got a minute, Cindy?"

"Sure. Something I can do for you?"

He lowers his voice and steps closer.

His nearness sends a strange tingling across my skin, and I have trouble catching my breath. Hopefully, I'm hiding it well.

"Every one of those pieces of jewelry ended up being stolen. So, thanks for that. The mayor is preparing a statement regarding the check, but he's admitted to being blackmailed."

"What for?"

Keith nods and smirks. "That's where the statement comes in. He's trying to admit he was being blackmailed and still cover his tracks."

"Do you think he had anything to do with Betty's death?" I tug at my apron strings as I wait for a reply.

"That's really what I came to tell you about. The mayor was looking like a great suspect until he provided an ironclad alibi. He was presiding over a town hall meeting that night. There were nearly forty witnesses who saw him leave after 10:30 p.m."

"That scream came from Betty's apartment around 8:30. So he's in the clear. That's good for him." I smile warmly.

Keith swallows and inhales sharply. "But not so great for you."

"Oh, right."

My shoulders slump, and I have the desperate urge to bake. "What about those women at the bingo hall? They were toasting Betty's death as though it was something to celebrate."

"Yeah, not a nice thing to do. However, if these are the same women I'm thinking of, Tawny, Claudette, and the rest, they were all victims of various petty thefts. Nothing serious enough to drive them to kill. We'll check their alibis for the time in question, but it sounds like they were simply being catty, not murderous."

I'm going to need to bake about twenty-four dozen cookies, or maybe one enormous cake, to get over this. "Wait! What about Todd Freeman? The guy at the laundromat. When I told him Betty was dead, he said it couldn't happen to a nicer woman. That seems pretty cold."

"He wasn't on our radar. I'll have a chat with him and see if he can account for his whereabouts. I'm doing everything I can, Cindy. Thanks again for the evidence."

Keith turns to leave, but I hate to see anyone walk away empty-handed. "Hey. Do you want to try one of the lemon-drop cookies with icing?"

He grins. "You don't have to ask me twice."

Returning from the baking area with half a dozen iced lemon-drop cookies, I hand the bag to Keith. "Here you go."

He accepts the cookies with a broad smile. "My mother always used to say the way to a man's heart is through his stomach. I never believed her until now."

My cheeks instantly flush. "That's a cute saying." My mouth feels dry as a popcorn ball.

Keith opens the package and pops a cookie in his mouth while I attempt to get my heart rate under control by asking more questions. "Oh, you didn't mention anything about that driver's license. That was Sherman in the photograph, wasn't it?"

He swallows, wipes the crumbs from the corner of his mouth, and frowns. "Yeah. That was an odd one. Sherman claims he had a falling out with his family and changed his name to put it all behind him. There's a deputy looking into it. At face value, it's not that suspicious. People change their names for a variety of reasons."

"Thanks again for keeping me in the loop, Keith."

"No problem, Cindy." He scoots past Justin's work area, waves to the handyman, and heads out.

Justin carefully scores and breaks a piece of glass before turning to me. "How do you know Keith so well? He's normally a pretty quiet guy."

Part of me doesn't want to mention the charges leveled against me, but honesty is my default. I can't help myself.

"I was the one who found Betty's body. I didn't know any better than to touch— Well, I'm the prime suspect."

Justin stops cold, and his jaw falls open like a baby bird hoping for a worm.

"I didn't do it. I'm innocent. I told Keith everything I know, and he believes me. That's why he's being so nice to me."

The handyman manages to close his mouth and

swallow. "Who in their right mind could think you had anything to do with a murder?"

"The deputy's name is Saul Rivera. Keith said he's kind of a hard-line sort of guy."

Justin throws his arms in the air. "Saul Rivera? That guy put me in the drunk tank overnight one time because I walked to my mailbox with an open beer. He claimed I was drunk in public or something. It was my first beer of the night. I was a long way from drunk, and — well, I would take those murder charges with a grain of salt."

"Thanks. That reminds me, Todd Freeman mentioned something about Betty reporting him for drunk and disorderly. Do you think she would've done that on purpose? To get him in trouble for something she knew wasn't true?"

Justin shrugs his narrow shoulders. "I didn't know Betty that well. Can't say I'm sorry. From what I've heard, she had a nasty streak."

"Yeah, I'm starting to wonder about that myself."

"I better get back to work, Cindy. I want to get everything finished for you today. It sure must be unsettling living next to a crime scene. I'll try to make you feel as safe as I can. If you like, I can install a decorative grate on the inside of the door. That way, if someone breaks the glass again, they won't be able to reach the lock from the outside."

"I wish I could say no, but all of this has made me feel unsafe for the first time in my life. That might be a good idea, Justin. Thank you."

I leave him to his work and return to the kitchen.

It might be time to make Cinnamon Roll's famous cranberry cheesecake. One of my papa's favorites.

CHAPTER 15

*J*USTIN KEEPS TO HIMSELF and only has
to interrupt me once for access to the
apartment to install that doggy door.

By the time I finish baking and icing all of my
cookies, he's wrapping up the final installation.

"Cindy, can I trouble you for a broom?"

"Sure. Just a minute." I grab a broom and
dustpan from the supply closet in the bakery and
return to the foyer.

"Thanks for taking care of this today. And
thanks for cleaning up after yourself."

He smiles as he sweeps. "No problem. I prefer
things tidy, and I figured you do too." Justin takes
the dustpan into the bakery and carefully dumps

the contents in the trash bin. "Do you think your dog wants to try the door?"

"Maybe. Artikoa, you wanna check out the access door?" Replacing the word doggy with access might be less insulting.

The white fox jumps up and heads up for the door leading directly outside. He sniffs carefully around the opening and tests the resistance with his head. In the blink of an eye, Arti shoots through the door and vanishes up the street.

Justin drops the broom and dustpan in a panic and heads for the door. "I'll get him, Cindy. I'm so sorry."

"Justin, wait. It's fine. Artikoa's totally self-sufficient. Don't worry about it. He'll be back. He's kind of obsessed with me." My soft chuckle will hopefully ease Justin's conscience.

He pats his chest and breathes a sigh of relief. "That's good to hear. I should've put his leash on before I— Well, come to think of it, he wasn't wearing a collar. Are you sure he's okay out there?"

"Yeah. Totally sure. He'd really hate a collar. And he's always been extremely well-behaved, so I let him get away with it." This whole skirting around the truth scenario is killing me. I need to get Justin out of here because I definitely can't tell an outright lie. "Cookie? Oh, right. Sworn off sugar. Sorry."

He grabs a small pad from his toolbox and makes his calculations. "I've written out the cost for each of the doggy doors, the metal grating, and the new pane of glass. And then there's a line item for labor. If it's too much, you can pay half now and half next week."

Taking the bill — I'm getting the hang of that word now — from Justin, I look at the pricing and the total and nod. "It seems fair. Hang on a minute."

Running up the stairs, I head over to the wooden chest and retrieve a handful of twenties. I'm learning to count the currency properly now, and I thumb through the papers twice to make sure I've gotten it right.

"Here you go, Justin. It was great to meet you. Thanks for doing such a good job."

He takes the money and smiles. "No problem. If you need anything else done, just talk to Frida. She knows how to get a hold of me."

Justin packs the rest of his tools into the back of his pickup truck and drives away.

Looks like the only thing left for me to do is deliver cookies to my neighbors. I had planned to take Artikoa with me, but it seems he's on an impromptu hunting trip. Personally, I'd like to know as little as possible about that.

Taking a large basket, I load the bags of peppermint, gingerbread, and lemon-drop cookies into careful rows.

My first stop will be Sherman's.

The hostess takes one look at me and shrugs her shoulders.

"I'll only be a minute. I wanted to give Sherman some thank-you cookies."

"Whatever. He's in the back."

When I push through the swinging door, Sherman is shouting at one of his employees as though it's the end of the world. I've seen elves make mistakes on toys before, but my father would never shout. He called them learning opportunities, and after careful conversation, he and the elf at fault would come up with a solution — together.

This is making me uncomfortable. I clear my throat loudly, hoping to get Sherman's attention.

He spins angrily, and when he catches sight of me, his expression doesn't change. "What do you want?"

"I was dropping off some cookies. Just wanted to say thanks again for letting me use your phone."

Finally, the lines on his forehead smooth. "No problem. Leave the cookies on the counter."

"Gingerbread, lemon-drop, or peppermint?"

The anger drains from him, and he blinks slowly. "Peppermint? Like chocolate cookies with peppermint pieces?"

"Exactly."

"I'll take those. My grandmother— Not important. Thanks. I gotta get back to work." The gruffness returns as quickly as it left.

"I thought you weren't close with your family." Oops. I shouldn't have said that out loud.

Sherman's mood darkens, and he steps toward me. "What do you know about my family?"

"Nothing. Sorry. Slip of the tongue."

I place the beribboned bag of peppermint cookies on the counter and hurry away. I hope I didn't screw up. If Sherman figures out Keith is sharing information with me— I don't want Keith to get in trouble.

Making my way down the street, I pass several businesses that are closed on Sunday. I suppose in a small town, the owners have to take some days off. Probably not enough employees to keep things open seven days a week. Not everyone has an entire village of elves.

There's a souvenir shop open that sells all kinds of Silver Shoals memorabilia. The owner is on the phone, but when I drop a bag of gingerbread cookies on the counter, she covers the mouthpiece, smiles, and whispers, "Thank you."

Nodding once, I slip away and continue with my deliveries. When I reach the bottom of the hill, I cross the street and head to the laundromat.

As I step inside, the aroma of soap floods my nostrils. The beige machines all stand in a row, and the cracked tan linoleum needs a scrub.

Todd Freeman sits at a scarred wooden desk, holding a nondescript mug in both hands. A couple of washing machines are chugging away, and there's clothing thumping 'round and 'round in a large dryer.

"Hi, Todd. I brought you some lemon-drop cookies."

Guilt flashes through his eyes as he sets his mug on the small desk and steps toward me.

"Thanks. Sorry about earlier. I've been bitten by dogs a couple times. Nothing against your dog, okay?"

"No problem. Enjoy your cookies."

He leans forward as he says thank you, and his breath smells strange. There's a sour, burning note that reminds me of Betty and her wine, but a little different.

"Todd, I really need to ask you a couple questions about Betty. Would that be okay?"

He slowly opens the bag of cookies, inhales deeply, and a strange softness falls across his face. "Sure. Ask whatever you want."

"Thanks. Where were you Friday night?"

"This past Friday?"

"Yep."

"I was at the town hall. The mayor's been talking about rezoning on Main Street which would eliminate the residential allowance. A lot of folks 'round here can only afford to have a shop on Main Street because they live above it. Take that away, and this town will dry up faster than a raisin in the sun."

"Gosh. That would be a problem. How did the vote go?"

"I was honestly kinda shocked at how close it was. I wish we would've had more of the retailers from Main Street there. I'm trying to get the word out. You know, make sure people show up next time, eh?"

"Well, I'm glad you were there, Todd. And I hope Sherman had a thing or two to say about rezoning."

"Sherman? He left before the mayor even finished his opening statement. He was sittin' five or six seats down from me. Looked like he got a text on his phone or something. He stormed out of there and never came back."

A slight chill creeps across my shoulders. "Do you remember what time he left?"

Todd pops another cookie in his mouth, chews thoughtfully, and nods. "Sure. Easy enough to remember, because the church bells started ringing. So that had to be 8:00. I figure he hadn't been gone but a minute or two . . . So yeah, 8:00 sounds right."

"Thank you, Todd. That's really helpful."

He lifts the half-empty bag of cookies and smiles. "Basket looks pretty full. I know a lot of folks are closed on Sunday." There's an unspoken question in his eyes.

"True. Then, I better give you another bag. Fresh cookies don't last forever."

A soft smile lifts the corners of his mouth as I hand him another bag of lemon-drop cookies. "Thanks again, Todd. I'm glad we had a chance to get acquainted."

He takes the bag, nods once, and smiles even more brightly. "Same here. Again, sorry about earlier."

I keep my thoughts about his *medicine* to my-self, smile politely, and leave.

I'm no expert at solving crimes. This is the very first one I've ever worked on. When I let myself stop and think, Sherman must be on the Naughty List for a reason. That strange driver's license, and now the news that he left the town hall early . . . Maybe I should call Keith.

The sun hangs low on the horizon, and a warm golden light illuminates the snow-covered great lake. From the vantage point on the sidewalk out-side my bakery, I can see for miles.

A worried yip echoes from behind, but comes a moment too late.

A rough bag slips over my head, and I drop my basket of cookies as I'm shoved into a vehicle. But it doesn't feel like a seat. It feels like the back part — the trunk!

CHAPTER 16

The car holding me captive moves slowly down the hill and turns. Then it turns again. It only takes a couple minutes before I lose all track of where I might be. If that yip was Artikoa, maybe he can use all of his wisdom to figure out a way to rescue me.

Otherwise, no one knows I'm missing.

Eventually the vehicle stops, and I hear what must be a key in the lock.

Rough hands yank me from the trunk and propel me in front of them. Reaching up, I try to clear whatever's covering my eyes, but something hard as steel pokes into my back.

"Leave it. You're my bargaining chip, and your only chance of survival is if you do what I say."

I don't know what kind of chip he plans to make out of me, but it sounds like my survival depends on following rules. Rule following isn't one of my strong suits, but I know how to get along when I need to.

The door creaks open, and I'm pushed into a room with musty odors, and it's not much warmer than it was outside.

The person propelling me shoves me onto a chair and ties my hands behind the back of the chair.

Moments later, I hear the crackle of a fire and can feel warmth in the distance. Must be about eight feet away. There's a fireplace in every home at the North Pole, and I'm a bit of an expert on chimneys. Despite my desire not to take over my father's business, I spent my entire childhood learning about it.

My captor paces in front of the fireplace.

Clearing my throat, I attempt to negotiate. "Excuse me. I wanted to mention, I don't know who you are. And I'm not sure why you tied me to this chair. If you let me go, that would be best for you. I won't say anything."

A gruff voice responds. "That's not an option. You know too much."

Hold on! I recognize the voice. He's struggling to hide it by making his voice deeper, but that's definitely Sherman. He's already said he won't let me go, so I'm not sure whether this is a good idea or a bad idea, but here goes.

"Sherman, please let me go. I don't know as much as you think I do. I was only delivering cookies. I don't know what you and your employee were arguing about, and I don't care."

"It's not about some stupid argument, you Christmas freak. I know you're looking into Betty's murder. You're not as dumb as that face on your sweater."

"I'm not a fan of people insulting my papa."

This comment brings a mocking scoff from Sherman.

"You can take this thing off my head now. I know who you are." My voice definitely sounds braver than I feel.

A moment later, the hood is ripped from my head, and Sherman Canton stands far too close. I can see a little spittle in the corner of his mouth as he says, "You should've kept your mouth shut. Minded your own business. Those murder charges never would've stuck on you. Now — now, I'm gonna have to silence you permanently."

That does not sound good. "If that really is your plan, why don't you tell me what actually happened? Must be difficult keeping it all secret."

He paces in front of the fireplace, still holding

the gun in his right hand. "Is that your official last request?"

Hoping against hope that it's not, it seems safest to let him think he's won. "Sure. If that's what you want to call it. I want to know what happened to Betty. She was my friend."

A wicked laugh erupts from his throat. "Betty was no one's friend. Betty was a manipulator. She used people and information to get what she wanted. I fell for it, too."

"Fell for what?"

"The helpful neighbor act. She was extremely friendly with me when I first moved to town. Then we started dating, casually, and I noticed little things."

"Like what?" My plan seems to be working. He's stopped pacing, and he's lost in thought. Not sure how long I can keep him distracted, but I remember reading *One Thousand and One Nights*. I might not have the skills of Scheherazade, but I'll do my best.

"Like how she always seemed to have a new piece of jewelry after we attended a party or went to dinner at a friend's. And sometimes, she would come into money. She claimed her parents were wealthy and helped her make ends meet, but I found out through a mutual friend that both her parents had passed away."

"Yeah. I heard that too. Someone was asking me who would empty out her apartment."

"Probably Ronnie. That's kind of the landlord's job when there's no one else. Cops took what they needed, thanks to you."

"What do you mean?"

"I got a buddy who's a deputy, okay? While you were the prime suspect, he was happy to feed me information so I could be in a position to get that property. Then they magically found my old driver's license — which Betty stole from me — and everything changed."

"I wasn't out to get you, Sherman. I was only trying to clear my name. I had no way of—"

"Plus, Betty was going to sublet to me until you showed up. Ever since you arrived in this town, you've ruined everything. You expect me to believe you weren't trying to make me look guilty? Good luck."

His anger is definitely on the rise. Time to place the focus back on Betty. "I'm sorry for the way things turned out, Sherman. It wasn't my intention. Why don't you tell me more about how things took such a bad turn with Betty?"

Sherman inhales, and his nostrils flare as he nods his head. "Yeah. I should've steered clear of her. She kept waffling on about subletting to me.

But I kinda liked her, and I thought she'd eventually see things my way."

"But she didn't. What happened when you went to her apartment that night?"

He waves his arms in the air, and for a moment, the gun is aimed in my direction. My captor doesn't seem to notice, and he turns to lean his arm and head against the mantle. "I went to have a talk. I swear to you. I didn't go over there with any plans to hurt Betty."

"I believe you, Sherman. What changed?"

"Betty. Betty changed."

"Something she said?" The ropes around my wrists hold tight despite my twisting and struggling while his attention is elsewhere. I'm making no progress on escape.

"She found that driver's license. I don't know whether she has some private investigator working for her or if she just has friends as dark and ugly as her, but she got to the truth."

"What truth?"

He spins and stares at me, slowly raising the gun. "As if you don't know."

"I don't know. The evidence I found, I turned over to Keith — Mr. Winters. He didn't tell me anything bad about the driver's license." Technically true.

Sherman lowers the gun and squints at me with

disbelief. "I got a record. I did a nickel in Clearwater for a ring of burglaries down south. I had to change my name when I got out of the state pen. I knew my old gang would be looking for me, and I wanted a fresh start. I learned my lesson. I wanted a new life."

Did my wrist move? I might be loosening the ropes. "Everyone deserves a second chance, Sherman. Why wouldn't Betty do that? Why wouldn't she let you have that?"

"Oh, Betty was going to give me my second chance. And she was even going to sublet her shop so I could set up my prep kitchen."

"Then why did she die?" There was more judgment in my voice than I intended.

"Don't talk to me like that. You barely knew her." He lifts the gun and glares. "She was going to blackmail me for fifty percent of my profits — not just the expansion — my whole restaurant. And she said if I didn't take the deal, she'd publish the driver's license and a story about me being a felon in the local newspaper, and all over the state. I couldn't let that happen, could I? Do you know the kind of people that are looking for me?"

"No, Sherman, I don't. How did the pen—?"

He levels the gun and stares straight down the barrel. "She wanted me to sign an agreement. Betty already had it drawn up. That horrible woman had been planning this for days. She handed me the pen, and — I lost it." Sherman rakes one hand through his messy ponytail, pulling chunks of blond hair loose and causing him to look mildly psychotic. "I wasn't in my right mind, okay? I just lost it."

"But if it was accidental, you could've called the police. You didn't. Why?"

He steps closer. "Why? Did you listen to anything I said, you ditzy broad? I'm an ex-con. Do you think the deputies would've given me the benefit of the doubt for even one minute?"

"Think about what you're doing now, Sherman. If you kill me, that only makes things worse."

"I don't see how much worse it could get. They'll put me away for life. Only got one of those. Two life sentences are meaningless. With you out of the way, I can tell my version of events. Maybe Betty attacked me. Maybe I was defending myself."

"Were you?"

He steps closer and shakes his head. "*Visiting* hours are over."

My movements are restricted by the ropes securing my wrists, but I can roll one hand over the other just enough to awaken a bit of my mother's gift of magic. By shifting the motions required to create a ball of light, I can increase the intensity and burn the rope off my wrists. Of course, this ignites my sweater, so as soon as my wrists come free, I yank my arms around and have to pat out the flames.

"What the—! Did you start a fire? You really are a freak!"

Getting to my feet, I put both hands on the wooden chair and summon another ball of flame. Once the chair ignites, I fling it hard at Sherman.

The gun is knocked from his hand into the fireplace.

I don't know very much about weapons, but something tells me that if he gets it back, it won't be good for me.

While Sherman screams and hollers, and trics to retrieve his gun from the flames, I dash out the front door.

He may have left his keys in the car, but that won't help me. I've never driven a car in my life. I don't mind the cold, and I'm good on my feet. Running seems like a great option.

As I race down the narrow road, headlights approach.

Waving my arms wildly, I stand in the middle of the road and jump up and down.

The car slides to a halt, and the driver's door opens.

"Help. Help me. Sherman Canton—"

Keith runs forward and throws an arm around me. Right behind him is Artikoa, yipping out a war cry.

"He's back in the cabin, Keith. You have to go get him. He's got a gun. Sherman did it. He did everything. And he grabbed me and—"

He softly brushes the side of my cheek. "We know. I got the real story behind the name change. Get in the car. And if I'm not back in five minutes, drive into town."

Keith pulls his gun and runs toward the cabin.

There's no time to tell him I don't know how to drive.

CHAPTER 17

"*A*RTI, I KNOW YOU'RE NOT REALLY A PET, but can I hold you in my lap? I'm still so scared."

Without a word, Artikoa crawls into my lap and nuzzles my chin.

Wrapping my arms around him, I stroke his soft fur and try to think happy thoughts of my papa and the North Pole.

Sirens blare behind us, and two police cars pull up, one on either side of Keith's vehicle.

Deputies leap out.

Three run toward the cabin, and one stops and opens the driver's side door. "Miss Claus, are you okay?"

"I'm okay. I burned my wrists a little, but you

better go help Keith. Sherman has a gun, and he's — he's really upset." The deputy closes the door and runs along to follow the others.

Artikoa and I wait in silence. There's gunfire, and I scream.

Moments later, two deputies emerge, propelling a handcuffed Sherman in front of them. He's bleeding from the shoulder.

They put him in their vehicle and drive away.

Still no sign of Keith.

"Should I go in? I know I don't have my mother's gift of healing, but—"

"This is a job for the humans, Cynthia. You've seen the dark side of these people, and I'm sorry for that. Those deputies are good men, and they take care of their own."

"What if Keith has been shot?"

Before Artikoa can answer, the last two deputies walk toward their vehicle.

I can't take it anymore. Opening the car door, I step out. "Where's Keith — Mr. Winters? Is he okay?"

The older deputy turns and steps toward me. The moonlight glints off his nameplate. Rivera. Oh dear.

"Miss Claus, on behalf of the department, let me apologize for the charges leveled against you. I can assure you they have all been dropped."

"Oh, thank you. I'm glad you found the actual killer."

"As are we. I'm not sure what you heard, but only one shot was fired, and that grazed Sherman Canton's shoulder. Keith is fine. He's collecting evidence."

Turning toward the cabin, I take a step, but Deputy Rivera grabs my shoulder. "Miss, I'd prefer if you didn't enter the crime scene."

This feels like the wrong time to remind him I was already *in* the crime scene and that the only reason it is a crime scene, to begin with, is because Sherman kidnapped me. Nope. This guy is definitely the kind of man who has to be handled like a hot cookie fresh from the oven. "Of course. I'll wait in the car."

"We can give you a ride back to town."

"That's okay. I'll wait here with my dog."

Deputy Rivera glances toward the car and nods. "Yeah, that's one heck of a dog. Winters claims that this mutt showed up on his doorstep, barking his head off until the ME got in his car. Then, this crazy compass of a canine was barking out directions. Like 'two barks' for left and 'one bark' for right or some nonsense. Anyway, Winters can tell you all about it. Wish I'd had a chance to say it sooner, but welcome to Silver Shoals, Miss Claus."

"Thank you, Deputy Rivera. I certainly hope things will settle down after this."

"Don't we all?" He turns and joins the other deputy. I watch their headlights disappear as he backs down the road from the cabin.

Before long, Keith joins us in the car. "Let me see your wrists."

Swallowing with difficulty, I extend both my arms in his direction, and he pops on his flashlight. "Let me get my first aid kit. We need to put something on those burns."

I wish I could tell him I'm a fast healer, and the blisters will be gone by tomorrow, but that would only raise more suspicion.

He returns with this first aid kit and gently rubs some salve on my wrists. "Cindy, how did the ropes catch fire?"

Well, this is a bit of a conundrum. I certainly can't tell him the truth. And lying—

"Yip."

"Everything happened so fast. Maybe I'll be able to remember better tomorrow."

Keith puts the ointment back in his first aid kit and turns in his seat to get a clear view of me and Artikoa. "There's something about you and that *dog*. I can't quite put my finger on it, but there's something."

My breath is shaky, and my heart rate picks up.

He turns his vehicle around and drives us back toward town. The moonlight sparkles off the thick drifts of snow on either side of the road, and it looks like a perfect night.

I've learned looks can be deceiving in the human world.

"Deputy Rivera said Artikoa showed up at your house."

"Yeah. It was the darndest thing. I was sitting down to supper, and I heard this commotion outside my front door."

"Wow. I always knew Artikoa was a great tracker, but that was some amazing work finding your house."

Keith chuckles. "The most amazing part is that it's not even my house. I'm renting a room from Deputy Rivera and his wife. I wanted to be close to the station, but couldn't afford to buy a place of my own."

"So, you answered the door and found Artikoa. Then what?" My heart is swelling with pride, but I want to hear Keith tell the story.

"He was jumping up and down and— I know this is going to sound crazy, Cindy, but I swear he was talking. It was sort of like a cross between a growl and a yodel, but I'm telling you — I heard words."

Arti growls softly in my lap, but I can't stifle

my chuckle. "He's pretty stubborn. And he seems to always know what he wants."

A soft yip of confirmation comes from the sly fox.

"Anyway, I got in my car, put him in the passenger seat, and somehow he got me out here. One time I made a wrong turn, and he growled so fiercely, I saw my life flash before my eyes."

I gasp, but Keith laughs heartily.

"I'm so glad you came. I'm not sure I could've run all the way back to town."

Keith glances over at me and smiles. "Oh, I bet all those gingerbread cookies would've fueled you for five or ten miles."

My cheeks flush under his gaze, and I laugh to hide my self-consciousness.

"Sherman confessed everything to me. Do you want me to come into the station to tell someone?"

"Oh, you can come down and make a statement in a couple of days — when you've recovered from all of this. No rush." He smiles and nods. "Todd Freeman came forward and told us that Sherman left the town hall meeting early. Between that and his kidnapping of you, we shouldn't have any trouble getting a confession out of him."

Once again, he grins at me. I struggle to stay calm, and return the smile.

"Would you like me to take you straight home,

or do you need some supper? You must be starved."

"I'm too upset to eat. I want to get back to my place and make a cranberry cheesecake. I know I'll feel better once I get started on a project."

"I gotta say, Cindy, you're absolutely made for baking. I've never tasted anything as delicious as your cookies. I'd love to have a piece of cheesecake."

"Oh, of course. It's always better after it sits in the refrigerator for a few hours. Maybe stop by tomorrow with cocoa — coffee."

"That sounds nice. I haven't got anything else going on. I'll see you about 10:00. Okay?"

I manage a nod, but the view steals my breath.

As we drive down the hill toward town, the entire village and the frozen water beyond glow with the luster of moonlight like a scene in a snow globe.

I made the right choice. Silver Shoals is the place for me. I can't wait to bake more treats!

"Here's your stop, miss."

Opening the door, I let Artikoa jump out first, and then I step to the curb. Arti bolts through the access door and disappears up the stairs.

I lean down and look across at Keith. "Thanks again for listening to Artikoa and coming to my rescue. Sherman was pretty unhinged."

"Yeah, he sure was. I'll see you tomorrow, Cindy."

"Right. See you tomorrow, Keith." Closing the door, I step back and wave.

The most terrifying night of my life has ended with a sweet twist. I don't know where things are headed, but it sure is nice to have a friend like Keith.

When I reach for the handle of the bakery and find the door unlocked, a momentary spasm of fear grips me. As I step in and see my purse and the basket of cookies setting on the floor just inside the doggy door, I know that one of the good Samaritans in town must've found them on the sidewalk after Sherman grabbed me. Sure was kind of them to have done the honest thing.

I retrieve my purse and lock the door behind me before entering the bakery to see if any of the cookies can be salvaged.

"It's so quiet, Arti. I don't think I even hear a mouse stirring."

"I should hope not." He sniffs indignantly.

As I gather the ingredients for Papa's favorite Christmas treat, Artikoa races around the bakery. "What are you doing?"

"I'm making a cranberry cheesecake. Then I'll be going to bed."

"On Christmas Eve?"

"It's Christmas Eve?" As soon as the words leave my lips, my internal Christmas clock confirms the fox's news.

"I was so distracted by the murder, and the kidnapping, and everything else! I haven't even hung up my stocking!"

"If you expect your father to make a stop, I suggest you get that stocking up before you start that cheesecake."

Racing up the steps two at a time, I burst into the apartment and rifle through my trunk. Arti and I double-check the Christmas lights, tinsel, and ornaments hanging from the light over our small table.

"Looks good, right?"

Artikoa sniffs sharply. "No tree."

"I didn't have time to get a tree or—

Hooking the loop of my stocking over an old nail in the wall next to my dresser, I breathe a sigh of relief. "It's no chimney, but I know Santa can work with it."

My teal-pink-and-gold handmade stocking is ready for Papa's visit.

Now, to make his favorite dessert!

CHAPTER 18

*L*ike children the world over, I must prepare for Santa.

I set a plate on the table between my two cozy velvet chairs. On my green plate, I place a generous slice of cranberry cheesecake.

Then I fill a cup with my secret-recipe hot cocoa, and put a candy cane in for stirring.

Artikoa joins me on the antique brass bed as we wait for Santa's arrival.

The hours slip away, and I drift in and out of dreamy sleep. Sometimes the visions are dark and involve Sherman and a cabin in the woods, while others are light and filled with happy memories of sugar-plums and the North Pole.

As you might've read in many a story, I fall fast asleep before the arrival of the reindeer and sleigh.

But when a soft voice calls my name, I'm awake in an instant. "Papa!"

Leaping out of bed, I run into my father's arms. The tears that fall are a combination of happiness, relief, and gratitude. "Sorry, Papa. I'm getting tears all over your beautiful, red-velvet suit."

"She's seen worse, sweetheart." He gestures to the chairs. "Sit down and tell me about your adventures in the human world."

As we get settled in the cozy chairs, Artikoa approaches. "Sir, may I make my report?"

Santa takes a large forkful of cranberry cheesecake and lifts it as a toast. "I love your reports, Artikoa. You've been greatly missed at the Pole. Please, enlighten me."

The pristine white fox nods. "I will let your daughter share the details of what has transpired since we left the dome. All I wish to say is that your faith was well-placed."

"Of course it was, Artikoa. You are my most trusted advisor."

The sly fox lifts his furry white head, and the small ears twist tightly together. "No, sir. Your faith in your daughter. It has been a joy to watch her among the humans. I suspected she was woefully ill-equipped for survival here, but it turns out I couldn't have been more wrong. Her generous, trusting nature is exactly what these people need. She's made friends where I saw only trouble, and I know that her kindness will change lives much as yours has, sir."

The unexpectedly kind words bring tears to my eyes, and I hop up to get a dishtowel to dry the salty drops from my cheeks.

As I return, Santa stirs his cocoa with the candy cane and smiles. "Your mother and I were worried. How could we not? We're parents. However, we believe you are the best parts of both of us, and with Artikoa's report, I shall return to the North Pole a proud father. We miss you every day, Marshmallow." He swallows with difficulty and strokes his fine beard. "You made the right choice. Now, let's hear your tale."

"Can I get you another slice of cheesecake first, Papa?"

He chuckles, and his round belly shakes. "Of course. Get one for yourself, too. We have all the time in the world." He offers a wink and a mischievous grin as I fetch our treats.

His expression grows dark when I share the details of the kidnapping, but he's pleased I've made friends in the community and wonders if Connie will share any more of her secrets with me.

"What do you mean, Papa?"

"You believe in ghosts, don't you, Marshmallow?"

"I never thought about it. I've never known anyone who's died. Do you think Connie's ghost is here — in the bakery?"

Papa glances toward the twinkling lights surrounding the window and smiles knowingly. "Connie loves baking as much as you. Perhaps the call of a kindred spirit will bring her joy in the afterlife."

"If you say so."

A moment of silence falls between us, and I fidget in my chair.

"Are you ready for your present, my dear?"

"I'm so ready, Papa."

His merry dimples deepen as he reaches into the big green sack at his feet. Before my eyes, he pulls out an enormous wooden sign.

"Special delivery for my daughter. Happy Birthday, Cynthia."

The sign has clearly been hand-carved with love. Little symbols in the scrollwork around the border serve as a secret message to me from the elves who worked on the project.

"Oh, it's beautiful."

He places it on the bed, and I stand to admire the details.

Pine trees carved so carefully they seem to

move in an invisible breeze, and then the beautiful letters of my bakery. Yuletide Me Over Bakery. And flying out of the "U" and over to the "T" is a miniature sleigh pulled by eight tiny reindeer, and Rudolph. "Is that you?"

Santa chuckles. "It is. The elves told me if you look closely, you can see every button on my coat."

I lean in and rely on my half-elven eyesight. "I can even see the texture of your velvet coat! And a bit of soot and ash — it's so lifelike."

He smiles. "The elves work miracles every day." Papa hugs his arm around my shoulders and kisses the top of my head. "I must finish the route — your route. Will you come for a visit soon?"

"I'm not sure, Papa. I have so much to do at my bakery, and I only understand a fraction of this human world. Maybe I can come home next Christmas."

"I'll let your mother know. If she can't wait until then, she has her ways."

Throwing both arms around my father's neck, I cry a few more tears into his fluffy white-as-snow beard. "Give Mama a hug for me when you get home. And tell every one of those elves how grateful I am for the sign."

"I will, Marshmallow." His eyes widen. "Goodness me! I have to make an extra stop to get those dried peppers for your mother."

"You don't want to end up on the Naughty List." I giggle until I can't breathe, and my father's hearty laughter fills my apartment with holiday cheer.

He turns to the wise fox. "You take care of my little girl, Artikoa."

The arctic fox sits tall and proper. "Yes, sir."

With that, my father lays his finger along the side of his nose and vanishes in a cloud of sparkles. A lovely little trick my mother taught him.

A moment later, the prancing and pawing of reindeer hooves on my roof is the only sign that Santa has returned to his sleigh.

I run to the window and gaze skyward. Just like in all the storybooks I read as a child, the reindeer and the sleigh holding my dear papa cross in front of the glowing moon, and I swear I can hear him shout "Merry Christmas to all, and to all a good night" as they disappear into the frosty air!

RECIPE: CINNAMON ROLL'S CHOCOLATE PEPPERMINT COOKIES

This is Cindy's favorite North Pole recipe!

These delicious cookies can be served warm or can be frozen for up to three weeks if you need to get ahead on your holiday baking. Thaw for forty-five minutes before serving.

Chocolate Peppermint Cookies
Ingredients
• 8 ounces of bittersweet baking chocolate, coarsely chopped
• ½ cup unsalted butter (*substitute oat milk butter or margarine*)
• 1 cup semi-sweet chocolate chips (*½ cup added now, ½ cup added to cool dough*)

• ½ cup crushed candy canes (*substitute hard peppermint candies if needed*)

• 6 Tablespoons granulated sugar (*substitute erythritol*)

• 3 large eggs

• 1 teaspoon vanilla extract (*substitute ½ teaspoon ground vanilla powder*)

• ½ teaspoon peppermint extract (*if you're a diehard, use 1 teaspoon*)

• 1 ½ cups all-purpose flour

• ¾ teaspoon baking powder

• ½ teaspoon salt (*Cindy prefers Cornish sea salt*)

Additional crushed candy cane pieces can be pressed into the tops of the warm cookies when you pull them from the oven.

Directions

1. In a double boiler, on medium heat, combine the bittersweet baking chocolate, your butter of choice, half of the semi-sweet chocolate chips, and the sugar. Stir until all chocolate is melted and the mixture is combined smoothly. Let cool at least 30 minutes.

2. Once the chocolate mixture is cool, add the half-cup of crushed candy canes and stir to combine.

3. Whisk the three eggs and the extracts to-

gether in a separate bowl. Add to the chocolate mixture and stir slowly, until completely combined.

4. In a separate bowl, combine the flour, baking powder, and salt. Whisk gently to combine. Add the dry mixture to your chocolate mixture. Stir to combine thoroughly.

5. Add the reserved half-cup of semi-sweet chocolate chips. Stir in. Cover and chill for up to two hours. You want the dough firm enough to shape.

6. When you remove the dough from the refrigerator, **PREHEAT the oven to 325°F**. Using a scoop or spoon, shape the dough into 1½-inch balls and place on parchment-lined cookie sheets.

7. Bake for 13 to 14 minutes. Cookies will puff up nicely. Remove from oven and let cool on tray for 5 minutes. At this point, you can press more crushed candy cane pieces onto the top of each cookie. Move cookies to wire racks to cool completely.

8. Makes approx. 2 dozen (depending on cookie size).

RECIPE: CONNIE'S GINGERBREAD COOKIES

Cindy swears this recipe is better than her North Pole version!

These chewy cookies are delicious with or without icing. They can be frozen for up to three weeks if you need to get ahead on your holiday baking. Cindy recommends freezing plain cookies and making a fresh batch of icing when you thaw them out. Thaw for forty-five minutes before serving (or 30 minutes before icing).

Gingerbread Cookies
Ingredients
• ¾ cup unsalted butter, softened (*substitute oat milk butter or margarine*)

- 1 cup dark brown sugar (*substitute Sukrin Gold*)
- ¼ cup blackstrap molasses (*substitute unsulphured molasses for a lighter cookie*)
- 2 teaspoons ground ginger
- 1 teaspoon ground cinnamon
- 1 teaspoon vanilla extract (*substitute ½ teaspoon ground vanilla powder*)
- ¼ teaspoon ground cloves
- ½ teaspoon salt (*Cindy prefers Cornish sea salt*)
- 1 large egg
- 2 cups all-purpose flour
- 1 teaspoon baking powder
- 1 teaspoon baking soda
- ¼ cup granulated sugar, for rolling (*substitute erythritol*)

For the icing

- 3 cups powdered sugar (*also known as confectioner's sugar*)
- 1 - 3 Tablespoons milk (*substitute water, if needed*)
- 1 teaspoon vanilla extract (*Cindy recommends CLEAR vanilla to keep the icing snow white*)
- *OPTIONAL: add a pinch of salt*

Directions

1. Preheat oven to 350°F and place parchment paper on cookie sheets. Set aside.

2. In your stand mixer bowl, cream your choice of butter and sugar together on medium speed until creamy.

3. Add molasses, spices, vanilla, and salt. Mix well.

4. Add egg, and mix thoroughly.

5. In a separate bowl, whisk together flour, baking powder, and baking soda.

6. Gradually mix dry ingredients into the batter until combined.

7. At this point, if the dough is sticky, chill for 30 minutes.

8. Using a scoop or spoon, shape the dough into 1½-inch balls, then roll through remaining granulated sugar until coated. Place on parchment-lined cookie sheets, leaving approx. 2-inch space between balls.

9. Bake for 12 to 14 minutes. Cookies will be golden and spread. Remove from oven and let cool on tray for 5 minutes. Move cookies to wire racks to cool completely.

10. Makes approx. 2 dozen (depending on cookie size).

For the icing

1. In a medium bowl, mix the powdered sugar, vanilla, (optional salt), and **1 Tablespoon** of the milk together. If the icing is too thick, add more milk, 1 tablespoon at a time, to thin it out. The consistency should hold a ribbon for 3 – 5 seconds.

   2. Fill a piping bag with your yummy icing and apply liberally!

RECIPE: YULETIDE LEMON-DROP COOKIES

These might be Keith Winters' favorite cookies!

These festive cookies are delicious with or without icing. They can be frozen for up to three weeks if you need to get ahead on your holiday baking. Cindy recommends freezing plain cookies and making a fresh batch of icing when you thaw them out. Thaw for forty-five minutes before serving (or 30 minutes before icing).

Lemon-Drop Cookies
Ingredients
For the cookies
- ½ cup unsalted butter, softened (*substitute oat milk butter or margarine*)
- ¾ cup granulated sugar (*substitute erythritol*)

• 1 large egg, room temperature (*cold eggs will shock this delicate batter and cause the butter to clump*)

• 2 Tablespoons lemon juice (*fresh squeezed is best!*)

• 1 - 2 Tablespoons lemon zest (*zest your lemon(s) first and then press for the juice*)

• 2¼ cups all-purpose flour

• 2 teaspoons baking powder

• ¼ teaspoon salt (*Cindy prefers Cornish sea salt*)

For the icing

• 3 cups powdered sugar (*also known as confectioner's sugar*)

• 2 - 4 Tablespoons lemon juice (*fresh squeezed is best!*)

• 1 - 2 Tablespoons lemon zest (*zest your lemon(s) first and then press for the juice*)

Directions

For the cookies

1. Preheat oven to 350°F and place parchment paper on cookie sheets. Set aside.

2. In your stand mixer bowl, cream your choice of butter and sugar together on medium speed until fluffy.

3. Add egg. Mix well.

4. Add lemon juice and zest, mix thoroughly.

5. In a separate bowl, whisk together flour, baking powder, and salt.

6. Gradually mix dry ingredients into the batter until combined. Dough will be sticky.

7. Using a scoop or spoon, scoop about 1 Tablespoon of lemon cookie dough and drop on parchment-lined cookie sheets, leaving approx. 2-inch space between cookies.

8. Bake for 13 to 15 minutes. Cookies will be light brown and firm. Remove from oven and let cool on tray for 5 minutes. Move cookies to wire racks to cool completely.

9. Makes approx. 3 dozen (depending on cookie size).

For the icing

1. In a medium bowl, mix the powdered sugar and **1 Tablespoon** of the lemon juice together. If the icing is too thick, add more lemon juice, 1 tablespoon at a time, to thin it out.

2. You can add the lemon zest to the icing or sprinkle over the freshly iced cookies. Cindy adds it to the icing to save time.

3. Dip the tops of the cooled cookies in the icing. Flip them back over, return to the cooling rack, and let the icing set.

RECIPE: SANTA'S FAVORITE CRANBERRY CHEESECAKE

Surprise Santa with cheesecake instead of cookies! Cindy loves making her father's favorite treat on Christmas Eve.

*****TIP: get all your ingredients out of the refrigerator about 1 hour ahead. This works best if everything is at room temperature.**

Cranberry Cheesecake
Ingredients
For the crumb crust
- ½ cup fine gingersnap cookie crumbs (*you can use more if you prefer a thicker crust*)
- 1 Tablespoon granulated sugar (*substitute erythritol*)
- 1 ¼ teaspoon ground cinnamon

- 1 teaspoon ground ginger
- ¼ teaspoon ground nutmeg
- Butter, for the sides and bottom of your spring-form pan (*substitute oat milk butter or margarine*)

For the cheesecake
- 5 large eggs, room temperature (*cold eggs do not get as fluffy*)
- 1 cup granulated sugar (*substitute erythritol*)
- ¾ cup small curd cottage cheese
- 12 ounces cream cheese, softened (*don't use "whipped" style*)
- Juice of one lemon, approx. 1 Tablespoon (*fresh squeezed is best!*)
- Zest of one lemon (*zest your lemon first and then press for the juice*)
- ½ cup cranberry sauce, with whole berries (*You can make your own or buy canned*)
- 1 cup sour cream
- Additional 1 cup cranberry sauce, with whole berries (*for topping and serving*)

Directions
For the crumb crust
1. In a medium mixing bowl, stir together the cookie crumbs, sugar, and spices until well mixed. (*To make the cookie crumbs, place cookies in a food proces-*

sor and process to fine crumbs OR place in a plastic storage bag and roll a rolling pin on top to create fine crumbs).

2. Butter the sides and bottom of an 8-inch or 9-inch spring-form pan.

3. Press the crumb mixture firmly into your spring-form pan and pop in the freezer for 10-15 minutes, so the crust can set before you add your cheesecake filling.

For the cheesecake

1. Preheat oven to 350°F.

2. In your stand mixer bowl, beat 5 eggs until thick and lemony in color.

3. Gradually add 1 cup of sugar, with mixer on low-medium speed.

4. Add cottage cheese and beat until combined.

5. Add softened cream cheese and beat until combined.

6. Stir in the zest and juice of one lemon.

7. Pour into cookie crumb-lined pan.

8. Drizzle ½ cup of cranberry sauce over the filling and gently drag a wooden skewer through the sauce to create a pattern in the cheesecake filling.

9. Bake for 1 hour, or until knife in center comes out clean.

10. Remove cheesecake from oven and spread 1

cup of thick sour cream evenly over the top. RE-TURN to 450°F oven for 5 minutes.

11. When cheesecake cools completely, (*Cindy recommends chilling in refrigerator overnight*), run a paring knife gently around the edge and remove the spring form. Decorate the top of the cake with additional cranberry sauce.

End of Book 1

But, more mysteries await...
Curl up with another case from the Christmas Catastrophe Mysteries series!

A NOTE FROM TRIXIE

I hope you have a wonderful holiday with your friends and family — anytime of year! Are you on the Nice List?

One of the best parts of bringing Cindy to life was the wonderful feedback from my early readers. Thank you to my alpha readers, Angel and Michael. HUGE thanks to my fantastic beta reader who gave me extremely useful and honest feedback: Nadine Peterse-Vrijhof. And big hugs to the world's best ARC Team – Trixie's Mystery ARC Detectives!

Thank you to my patient editor Philip Newey! Some authors dread edits, but it is always a pleasure to work with Philip, and I look forward to many more. I'd also like to give heaps of gratitude to Roxx at Proof Perfect for the stellar proofing! Any remaining errors are my own.

I love baking! When my grandmother passed, I was lucky enough to inherit her recipe box. What a treasure! It brings a smile to my face every time I'm able to share one of her special bakes with you.

If you enjoyed this mystery, you can find more of my humorous paranormal cozies in the Mitzy Moon Mysteries, Harper and Moon Investigations, the Magical Renaissance Faire Mysteries, and the Mysteries of Moonlight Manor

We're so glad you chose to visit Silver Shoals. I hope you'll continue to hang out with us.

Trixie Silvertale (November 2023)

APPLE DUMPLING MURDER

Santa's daughter is happily settling into her life as a baker. Could a fresh murder burn her biscuits?

Cindy Claus loves exploring the human world and baking amazing treats. She should be bubbling over when her aging landlord takes her under his wing and promises to leave her the bakery in his will. However, before she can stir up a celebration, her patron collapses, dead, like a bad soufflé.

With suspicion instantly falling on the budding baker, Cindy must rely on her fragile new friendships and her father's trusted arctic fox. She'll have to sidestep local law enforcement as she gathers crumbs, and one wrong move could crush her dreams...

Can Cindy find the proof she needs, or will this villain punch down her last hope?

Apple Dumpling Murder is the second book in the festive paranormal cozy series, Christmas Catastrophe Mysteries. If you like kind-hearted heroines, furry sidekicks, and a dash of mistletoe magic, then you'll love Trixie Silvertale's seasonal secrets.

Buy *Apple Dumpling Murder* to blind bake a killer today!

Features recipes from Cindy's bakery!

Grab your next read here!
readerlinks.com/l/5211921

Scan this QR Code with the camera on your phone. You'll be taken right to the next Christmas Catastrophe Mysteries *adventure!*

SPECIAL INVITATION . . .

In between Christmas Catastrophe Mysteries, you can come visit Pin Cherry Harbor!

Get access to the Exclusive Mitzy Moon Mysteries character quiz – free!

Find out which character you are in Pin Cherry Harbor and see if you have what it takes to be part of Mitzy's gang.

This quiz is only available to members of the Paranormal Cozy Club, Trixie Silvertale's readers group.

Visit the link below to join the club and get access to the quiz:

Join Trixie's Club

http://trixiesilvertale.com/paranormal-cozy-club/

Once you're in the Club, you'll also be the first to receive updates from Pin Cherry Harbor and access to giveaways, new release announcements, behind-the-scenes secrets, and much more!

Scan this QR Code with the camera on your phone. You'll be taken right to the page to join the Club!

THANK YOU!

Trying out a new book is always a risk. Thank for rolling the dice with Cindy Claus. If you loved the book, the sweetest thing you can do (*even sweeter than peppermint hot chocolate*) is to leave a review so other readers will take a chance on Cindy and Artikoa.

Don't feel you have to write a book report. A brief comment like, "Can't wait to read the next book in this series!" will help potential readers make their choice.

★★★★★

Leave a quick review HERE
https://readerlinks.com/l/3697052

★★★★★

Thank you kindly, and I'll see you in Silver Shoals!

Blades and Bridesmaids: Paranormal Cozy Mystery

Scones and Tombstones: Paranormal Cozy Mystery

Vandals and Yule Scandals: Paranormal Cozy Mystery

Harper and Moon Investigations

Ropes and Last Hopes: Paranormal Cozy Mystery

Bells and Bombshells: Paranormal Cozy Mystery

Rodeo Clowns and Shakedowns: Paranormal Cozy Mystery

Stiffs and Petroglyphs: Paranormal Cozy Mystery

Fatal Wines and Valentines: Paranormal Cozy Mystery

April Curses and May Hearses: Paranormal Cozy Mystery

Wheels and Dirty Deals: Paranormal Cozy Mystery

Scripts and Empty Crypts: Paranormal Cozy Mystery

Christmas Catastrophe Mysteries

Peppermint Cookie Murder: Paranormal Cozy Mystery

Apple Dumpling Murder: Paranormal Cozy Mystery

Linzer Cookie Murder: Paranormal Cozy Mystery

Chocolate Crinkle Cookie Murder: Paranormal Cozy Mystery

...more to come!

MAGICAL RENAISSANCE FAIRE MYSTERIES

Explore the world of Coriander the Conjurer. A fortune-telling fairy with a heart of gold!

Book 1:

All Swell That Ends Spell – A dubious festival. A fatal swim. Can this fortune-telling fairy herald the true killer?

Book 2:

Fairy Wives of Windsor – A jolly Faire. A shocking murder. Can this furtive fairy outsmart the killer?

Book 3:

Double Double Royal Trouble – When a treat-peddling witch is found dead, will this cursed faire crumble?

MYSTERIES OF MOONLIGHT MANOR

Join Sydney Coleman and her unruly ghosts, as they solve mysteries in a truly haunted mansion!

Book 1: ***Moonlight and Mischief*** – She's desperate for a fresh start, but is a mansion on sale too good to be true?

Book 2: ***Moonlight and Magic*** – A haunted Halloween tour seem like the perfect plan, until there's murder...

Book 3: ***Moonlight and Mayhem*** – An unwelcome visitor. A surprising past. Will her fire sale end in smoke?

ABOUT THE AUTHOR

USA TODAY Bestselling author Trixie Silvertale grew up reading an endless supply of Lilian Jackson Braun, Hardy Boys, and Nancy Drew novels. She loves the amateur sleuths in cozy mysteries and obsesses about all things paranormal. Those two passions unite in all her paranormal cozy mysteries, and she's thrilled to write them and share them with you.

When she's not consumed by writing, she bakes to fuel her creative engine and pulls weeds in her herb garden to clear her head (*and sometimes she pulls out her hair, but mostly weeds*).

Greetings are welcome:
trixie@trixiesilvertale.com

facebook.com/TrixieSilvertale

instagram.com/trixiesilvertale

bookbub.com/authors/trixie-silvertale